"You still wish you hadn't been cornered into coming here tonight."

"Naturally."

"Because you'd hoped you'd never set eyes on me again."

Octavia flushed. "That, too."

"And you'd like very much for us both to forget our first encounter ever happened."

"Yes," she said. "Yes, I would."

"Very understandable. And for me, anyway, quite impossible. The vision of you rising like Venus from the waves will always be a treasured memory." Jago paused. "And I like your hair loose."

She was burning all over now. It wasn't just what he'd said, but the way he'd looked at her across the table, as if her dress—her clothing—had ceased to exist under his gaze. As if her hair tumbling around her shoulders was her only covering. And as if he knew that her nipples in some damnable way were hardening into aching peaks inside the lacy confines of her bra.

But if her skin was fire, her voice was ice. "Fortunately, your preferences are immaterial to me."

Sara Craven

—

Seduction Never Lies

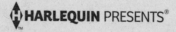

HARLEQUIN PRESENTS®

Recycling programs
for this product may
not exist in your area.

ISBN-13: 978-0-373-13220-1

SEDUCTION NEVER LIES

First North American Publication 2014

Copyright © 2014 by Sara Craven

Printed in U.S.A.

Seduction Never Lies

CHAPTER ONE

OCTAVIA DENISON FED the last newsletter through the final letter box in the row of cottages and, with a sigh of relief, remounted her bicycle and began the long hot ride back to the Vicarage.

There were times, and this was one of them, when she wished the Reverend Lloyd Denison would email his monthly message to his parishioners instead.

'After all,' as Patrick had commented more than once, 'Everyone in the village must have a computer these days.'

But her father preferred the personal touch, and when Tavy came across someone like old Mrs Lewis longing for a chat over a cup of tea because her niece was away on holiday, and who certainly had no computer or even a mobile phone, she supposed wryly that Dad had a point.

All the same, this was not an ideal day for a cycle tour of the village on an old boneshaker.

For once, late May had produced a mini-heatwave with cloudless skies and temperatures up in the Seventies, which had also managed to coincide with Greenbrook School's half-term holiday.

Nice for the kids, thought Tavy as she pedalled but, for her, it would be business as usual tomorrow.

Her employer, Eunice Wilding, paid her what she considered was the appropriate rate for a young and unqualified school secretary, but she expected, according to the local saying, 'her cake for her ha'penny'.

But at the time the job had seemed a lifeline in spite of the poor pay. One small ray of light in the encircling darkness of the stunned grief she shared with her father at her mother's sudden death from a totally unsuspected heart condition.

He'd protested, of course, when she'd announced she was giving up her university course to come home and keep house for him, but she'd read the relief in his eyes, swallowed her regrets, and set herself to rebuilding both their lives, cautiously tackling the parish tasks that her mother had fulfilled with such warmth and good humour, while discovering that, in Mrs Wilding's vocabulary, 'assistant' was another word for 'dogsbody'.

But in spite of its drawbacks, the job enabled her to maintain a restricted level of independence and pay a contribution to the Vicarage budget.

In return, she was expected to put in normal office hours, five and a half days a week, with just a fortnight's holiday taken in two weekly instalments in spring and autumn, and far removed from the lengthy vacations enjoyed by the teaching staff.

And half-term breaks did not feature either, so this particular afternoon was a concession, while Mrs Wilding conducted her usual staff room inquisition into the events of the past weeks, and outlined the progress she expected in the next half.

It was her ability to achieve these targets that had made Greenbrook School an undoubted success in spite of its high fees. Mrs Wilding herself did not teach, calling herself the Director rather than the headmistress, but she had a knack for picking those that could, and even the most unpromising pupils were given the start they needed.

When she eventually retired, the school would continue to flourish under the leadership of Patrick, her only son, who'd returned from London the previous year to become a partner in an accountancy firm in the nearby market town, and who already acted as Greenbrook's part-time bursar.

And his wife, when he had one, would also have a part to play, thought Tavy, feeling an inner glow that had nothing to do with the sun.

She'd known Patrick all her life of course, and he'd been the object of her first early teen crush. While her school friends giggled and fantasised over pop stars and soap actors, her sole focus had been the tall, fair-haired, blue-eyed Adonis who lived in her own village.

Although it might as well have been one of the moons of Jupiter for all the notice he took of her. She could remember basking for weeks in the memory of a casual 'Thanks' when she'd been ball girl for his final match in the annual village tennis tournament. Could recall the excitement building as the university vacations approached and she knew he would be home, but also crying herself to sleep when he spent his holidays elsewhere, as he often did.

But then real life in the shape of public examinations and career choices intervened and took priority, so that when she heard her father mention casually to her mother that Patrick was off to the States for some form of post-graduate study, the worst she had to suffer was a small pang of regret.

Since that time, he'd come back only for fleeting visits, and the last thing Tavy expected was that he would ever return to live in the area. Yet six months ago that was exactly what had happened.

And the first she'd known of it was when his mother brought him one afternoon into the cubbyhole which served as her office.

She'd said rather stiffly, 'Patrick, I don't know if you remember Octavia Denison…'

'Of course, I do.' His smile seemed to reach out and touch her, as she'd seen it do so often to others in the past. But, until that moment, never to her. 'We're old friends.' Adding, 'You look terrific, Tavy.'

She'd felt the swift colour burn in her face. Fought to keep her voice steady as she returned, 'It's good to see you again, Patrick.'

Knowing that she had not bargained for precisely how good. And feeling a swift stab of anxiety in consequence.

After that, he seemed to make a point of popping in to see her whenever he was at the school, perching on the corner of her desk to chat easily as if that past friendship had really existed, and she hadn't simply been 'that skinny red-haired kid from the Vicarage' as one of the girls in his crowd had once described her, loudly enough to be overheard.

Tavy had remained on her guard, polite but not encouraging, her instinct telling her that Mrs Wilding was unlikely to approve of such fraternisation. Not even sure that she approved of it herself, even if the bursarship gave him an excuse for being there.

So, when Patrick eventually invited her to have dinner with him, her refusal was immediate and definite.

'But why?' he asked plaintively. 'You do eat, don't you?'

She hesitated. 'Patrick, I work for your mother. It wouldn't be—appropriate for you to take out the hired help.'

Besides I need this job, because finding another in the same radius is by no means a certainty...

He snorted. 'For heaven's sake, what century are we living in? And Ma will be cool about it, I guarantee.'

But she remained adamant, only to discover that he was adopting a similar stance. And, finally, at the third time of asking, and in spite of her lingering misgivings, she agreed.

It occurred to her while she was getting ready, searching the wardrobe for the one decent dress she possessed and praying it still fitted, that she hadn't actually been out with a man since those few short months at university when she'd had a few casual but enjoyable dates with a fellow student called Jack.

Looking back, she could see that these might have developed into something more serious, if Fate hadn't intervened with such devastating cruelty.

Since then nothing—and no one.

For one thing, there were few single and available men in the neighbourhood. For another, coping with her job, plus the cooking and housework at the Vicarage and helping out with parish duties left her too tired to go looking, even if she'd had the time or inclination.

She could only hope that Patrick hadn't tuned into this somehow and invited her out of pity.

If so, he'd kept it well-hidden during an evening it still made her smile to remember. He'd taken her to a small French restaurant in Market Tranton where they'd begun with a delicious garlicky pâté before moving on to *confit du canard,* served with green beans and a *gratin dauphinois,* with a seriously rich chocolate mousse to complete the meal. All washed down with a soft, fruity Bergerac wine.

A meal from the Dordogne region, he'd told her, and probably the only one she'd ever taste, she thought later, as she drifted off to sleep.

After that, they'd started seeing each other on a regular basis, although when they encountered each other in working hours, it was always strictly business. And in spite of his assurances, Tavy wasn't at all sure that her employer was actually aware of the whole situation. Certainly Mrs Wilding made no reference to it, but maybe that was because she considered it unimportant. A temporary aberration on Patrick's part which would soon pass.

Except it showed no sign of doing so, although so far he'd made no serious attempt to get her into bed, as she'd half expected. And, perhaps, wanted, having no real wish to remain the only twenty-two-year-old virgin in captivity.

And while she knew she could not expect her father to approve, he'd been enough of a realist to impose no taboos in his pre-university advice. Just a quietly expressed hope that she would always maintain her self-respect.

So, sleeping with a man with whom she shared a settled relationship could hardly damage that, she told herself. In many ways it would be an affirmation. A promise for the future.

Although all their meetings were still taking place well away from the village.

When, at last, she'd tackled him about this, he'd admitted ruefully that he'd been deliberately keeping the situation under wraps. Saying that his mother had a lot on her mind at the moment, and he was waiting for the right moment to tell her about their plans.

If, of course, there was ever going to be a right moment, Tavy had thought, sighing inwardly.

Mrs Wilding cultivated sweetness like other people cultivate window-boxes. For outward show.

How she would react if and when she discovered her assistant might one day be transformed from drudge to daughter-in-law was anyone's guess, but Tavy's money would be on 'badly'.

But I'll worry about that when I have to, she thought, putting up a hand to wipe away the sweat trickling down into her eyes.

The first inkling she had that a vehicle was behind her came with a loud blast on its horn. Gasping, she wobbled precariously for a moment then got her bike back under control before it veered into the ditch.

The car that had startled her, a sleek open-top sports model, overtook her and drew up a few yards ahead.

'Hi, Octavia.' The driver turned to address her, languidly pushing her designer sunglasses up on to smooth blonde hair. 'Still using that museum piece to get around?'

Striving to recover her temper along with her balance, Tavy groaned inwardly.

Fiona Culham that was, she thought with resignation. She would have recognised those clipped brittle tones anywhere. Just not anticipated hearing them round here any time soon, and would have preferred it kept that way.

Reluctantly, she dismounted and pushed her cycle level with the car. 'Hello, Mrs Latimer.' She kept her tone civil but cool, reflecting that although Fiona was only two years her senior, the use of Christian names had never been reciprocal. 'How are you?'

'I'm fine, but you're a little behind the times. Didn't you know that I'm using my maiden name again now that the divorce is going through?'

Heavens to Betsy, thought Tavy in astonishment. You were only married eighteen months ago.

Aloud, she said, 'No I hadn't heard, but I'm very sorry.'

Fiona Culham shrugged. 'Well, don't be, please. It was a hideous mistake, but you can't win them all.'

The hideous mistake—an enormous London wedding to the wealthy heir to a stately home, with minor royalty present—had been plastered all over the newspapers, and featured in celebrity magazines. The bride, described as radiant, had apparently been photographed before she saw the error of her ways.

'A little long-distance excitement for us all,' the Vicar had remarked, at the time, laying his morning paper aside. He sighed. 'And I can quite see why Holy Trinity, Hazelton Magna, would not have done for the ceremony.'

And just as well, Tavy thought now, knowing how seriously her father took the whole question of marriage, and how grieved he became when relationships that had started out with apparent promise ended all too soon on the rocks.

She cleared her throat. 'It must be very stressful for you. Are you back for a holiday?'

'On the contrary,' Fiona returned. 'I'm back for good.' She looked Tavy over, making her acutely aware that some of her auburn hair had escaped from its loose topknot and was hanging in damp tendrils round her face. She also knew that her T-shirt and department store cut-offs had been examined, accurately priced and dismissed.

Whereas Fiona's sleek chignon was still immaculate, her shirt was a silk rainbow, and if Stella McCartney made designer jeans, that's what she'd be wearing.

'So,' the other continued. 'What errand of mercy are you engaged with today? Visiting the sick, or alms for the poor?'

'Delivering the village newsletter,' Tavy told her expressionlessly.

'What a dutiful daughter, and no time off for good behaviour.' Fiona let in the clutch and engaged gear. 'No doubt I'll see you around. And I really wouldn't spend any more time in this sun, Octavia. You look as if you've reached melting point already.'

Tavy watched the car disappear round a bend in the lane, and wished it would enter one of those time zones where people mysteriously vanished, to reappear nicer and wiser people years later.

Though no amount of time bending would improve Fiona, the spoiled only child of rich parents, she thought. It was Fiona who'd made the skinny red-haired kid remark, while Tavy was helping with the tombola at a garden party at White Gables, her parents' home.

Norton Culham had married the daughter of a millionaire, and her money had helped him buy a rundown dairy farm in Hazelton Parva and transform it into a major horse breeding facility.

Success had made him wealthy, but not popular. Tolerant people said he was a shrewd businessman. The less charitable said he was a miserable, mean-spirited bastard. And his very public refusal to contribute as much as a penny to the proposed restoration fund for Holy Trinity, the village's loved but crumbling Victorian church had endeared him to no one. Neither had his comment that Christianity was an outdated myth.

'It's a free country. He can think what he likes, same as the rest of us,' said Len Hilton who ran the pub. 'But there's no need to bellow it at the Vicar.' And he added an uncomplimentary remark about penny-pinching weasels.

But no pennies had ever been pinched where Fiona was concerned, thought Tavy. After she'd left one of England's most expensive girls' schools, there'd been a stint in Switzerland learning cordon bleu cookery, among other skills that presumably did not include being pleasant to social inferiors.

However, Fiona had been right about one thing, she thought, easing her T-shirt away from her body as she remounted her bike. She was indeed melting. However there was a cure for that, and she knew where to find it.

Accordingly when she reached a fork in the lane a few hundred yards further on, she turned left, a route which would take her past the high stone wall which encircled the grounds of Ladysmere Manor.

As she reached the side gate, hanging sadly off its hinges, she saw that the faded 'For Sale' sign had fallen off and was lying in the long grass. Dismounting, Tavy picked it up and propped it carefully against the wall. Not that it would do much good, she acknowledged with a sigh.

The Manor had been on the market and standing empty and neglected for over three years now, ever since the death of Sir George Manning, a childless widower. His heir, a distant cousin who lived in Spain with no intention of returning, simply arranged for the contents to be cleared and auctioned, then, ignoring the advice of the agents Abbot and Co, put it up for sale at some frankly astronomical asking price.

It was a strange mixture of a house. Part of it was said to date from Jacobean times, but since then successive genera-

tions had added, knocked down, and rebuilt, leaving barely
a trace of the original dwelling.

Sir George had been a kindly, expansive man, glad to
throw his grounds open to the annual village fête and allow
the local Scouts and Guides to camp in his woodland, and
whose Christmas parties were legendary.

But without him, it became very quickly a vacant and
overpriced oddity, as his cousin refused point blank to offer
the same hospitality.

At first, there'd been interest in the Manor. Someone was
said to want it for a conference centre. A chain of upmarket nursing homes had made an actual offer. A hotel group
was mentioned and there were even rumours of a health spa.

But the cousin in Spain obstinately refused to lower his
asking price or consider offers, and gradually the viewings
petered out and stopped, reducing the Manor from its true
place as the hub of the village to the status of white elephant.

Tavy had always loved the house, her childish imagination transforming its eccentricities into a place of magic,
like an enchanted castle.

Now, as she squeezed round the gate and began to pick
her way through the overgrown jungle that had once been a
garden, she thought sadly that it would take not just magic
but a miracle to bring the Manor back to life.

Over the tangle of bushes and shrubs, she could see the
pale shimmering green of the willows that bordered the lake.
At the beginning, volunteers from the village had come and
cleared the weeds from the water, as well as mowing the
grass and cutting back the vegetation in front of the house,
but an apologetic letter from Abbot and Co explaining that
there was no insurance cover for accidents had put a stop
to that.

But the possibility of weeds was no deterrent for Tavy.
She'd encountered them before in previous summers when
the temperature soared, and all that mattered was the pros-

pect of cool water against her heated skin. And because she always had the lake to herself, she never had to bother with a swimsuit.

It had become a secret pleasure, not to be indulged too often, of course, but doing no harm to anyone. In a way, she felt as if her occasional presence was a reassurance to the house that it had not been entirely forgotten.

And nor was the Lady, who'd been there for nearly three hundred years, and therefore must find all these recent months very dull without company, standing naked on her plinth looking down at the water, one white marble arm concealing her breasts, her other hand chastely covering the junction of her thighs.

Tavy had always been thankful that the statue hadn't been sent to the saleroom, along with Sir George's wonderful collection of antique musical boxes, and his late wife's beautifully furnished Victorian doll's house.

You had a lucky escape there, Aphrodite or Helen of Troy, or whoever you're supposed to be, she said under her breath as she took off her clothes, putting them neatly on the plinth before unclipping her hair. Because the lake wouldn't be the same without you.

The water wasn't just cool, it was very cold, and Tavy gasped as she took her first cautious steps from the sloping bank. As she waded in more deeply, the first shock wore off, the chill becoming welcome, until with a small sigh of pleasure, she submerged completely.

Above her, she could see the sun on the water in a dazzle of green and gold and she pushed up towards it, throwing her head back as she lifted herself above the surface in one graceful joyous burst.

And found herself looking at darkness. A black pillar against the sun where there should only have been blanched marble.

She lifted her hands, almost frantically dragging her hair

back from her face, and rubbing water from the eyes that had to be playing tricks with her.

But she wasn't hallucinating. Because the darkness was real. Flesh and blood. A man, his tall, broad-shouldered, lean-hipped body emphasised by the close-fitting black T-shirt and pants he was wearing, who'd appeared out of nowhere like some mythical Dark Lord, and who was now standing in front of the statue watching her.

'Who the hell are you?' Shock cracked her voice. 'And what are you doing here?'

'How odd. I was about to ask you the same.' A low-pitched voice, faintly husky, its drawl tinged with amusement.

'I don't have to answer to you.' Realising with horror that her breasts were visible, she sank down hastily, letting the water cover everything but her head and shoulders. 'This is private property and you're trespassing.'

'Then that makes two of us.' He was smiling openly now, white teeth against the tanned skin of a thin tough face. Dark curling hair that needed cutting. A wristwatch probably made from some cheap metal and a silver belt buckle providing the only relief from all that black. 'And I wonder which of us is the most surprised.'

It occurred to her that he looked like one of the travellers who'd been such a nuisance over the winter.

They must have come back, looking for more scrap metal, thought Tavy, treading water. And he's probably here to nick the lead from the Manor roof.

It was difficult to speak with dignity under the circumstances, but she gave it her best shot.

'If you leave right now, I won't report this to the authorities. But the place is being watched. There are CCTV cameras, so you won't get away with a thing.'

'Thanks for the warning. Although they must be well-hidden because I haven't spotted one of them.' Casually, he moved her pile of clothing to one side, and sat down on the plinth. 'Perhaps you could show me a safe exit out of here. The same way you got in, maybe.'

'And I suggest you go back the way you came, and waste no time about it.' Tavy could feel her teeth starting to chatter and couldn't be sure whether she was getting cold or just nervous. Or both.

'On the other hand,' he said. 'This is a charming spot and I'm in no particular hurry.'

It's both, thought Tavy. No doubt about it. Plus the kind of hideous jaw-clenching embarrassment you only encounter in nightmares.

'However, I am,' she said, trying to speak levelly. Reasonably. 'So I'd really like to put my clothes back on.'

He indicated the pile of garments beside him. 'Be my guest.'

'But without you looking on.' *Because she'd rather freeze or get caught in the weeds and drown than have to walk out of the water naked in front of him.*

He was smiling again. 'And how do you know I wasn't watching while you took them off?' he enquired gently.

She swallowed past the sudden tightness in her throat. 'Were—you?'

'No.' He had the unmitigated gall to make it sound regretful. 'But I'm sure there'll be other occasions,' he added unforgivably, then paused as soft chimes sounded, reaching into his pocket for his mobile phone.

'Hi,' he said. 'Yes, everything's fine. I'll be with you shortly.'

He disconnected and rose. 'Saved by the bell,' he commented.

'You certainly have been,' Tavy said curtly. 'I was considering charging you with sexual harassment.'

'Just for a little gentle teasing?' He shook his head. 'I don't think so. Because you'd have to tell the police exactly where you were and what you were doing. And somehow, my little trespasser, I don't think you'd want that.'

He blew her a kiss. 'See you around,' he said and sauntered off without a backward glance.

CHAPTER TWO

For a while Tavy stayed where she was, waiting until she could be totally sure he had gone. Then, and only then, she swam to the bank and climbed out, her legs shaking under her.

She would normally have dried off in the sun, but this time she dragged her clothes on over her clammy skin, wincing at the discomfort, but desperate to get away. Cursing herself inwardly for the impulse which had brought her here. Knowing that this special place had been ruined for her for ever, and that she would never come back.

And she didn't feel remotely refreshed. Instead, she felt horribly disturbed, her heart going like a trip-hammer. And dirty. Also sick.

See you around...

That was the second time someone had said that to her today, and her silent response had been the same to each of them—'Not if I see you first.'

Well, she probably couldn't avoid Fiona Culham altogether, but, after this recent encounter, she could let the police know that there were undesirables in the neighbourhood.

And gentle teasing be damned, she thought, pulling on her T-shirt and sliding her damp feet into their shabby canvas shoes. Remembering the wide shoulders and the muscularity of his arms and chest, she knew she could have been in real danger. Because if he'd made a move on her, there was no guarantee she'd have been strong enough to fight him off.

Trying to make her wet hair less noticeable, she dragged it back from her face and plaited it into a thick braid, fingers all thumbs, securing it with one of the elastic bands that had been round the newsletters.

Now she felt more or less ready to face the outside world again. And some, but not all, of the people in it.

When she got back to the gate, she was almost surprised to find her bicycle where she'd left it. Dad had always dismissed the old saying about bad things happening in threes as a silly superstition, but it occurred often enough to make her wonder. Only not this time, it seemed, she thought with a sigh of relief, as she cycled off, determined to put as much distance as she could between herself and Ladysmere Manor with as much speed as possible.

When she got back to the Vicarage, she found her father in the kitchen, sitting at the table with a pot of tea and the crossword, plus the substantial remains of a rich golden-brown cake.

She said lightly, 'Hi, darling. That looks good.'

'Ginger cake,' said Mr Denison cheerfully. 'I had some at the WI anniversary tea the other week and said how delicious it was, so the President, Mrs Harris baked another and brought it round.'

'You,' Tavy said severely, 'are spoiled rotten. I suppose they've guessed that my baking sets like concrete in the bottom of the tin?'

His smile was teasing. 'One Victoria sponge that had to be prised loose. Since then—straight As.'

'Flatterer,' said Tavy. She paused. 'Dad, have you heard if the travellers have come back?'

'It's not been mentioned,' he said with faint surprise. 'I

confess I'd hoped they were safely settled on that site at Lower Kynton.'

You can say that again, thought Tavy, her mind invaded by an unwanted image of a dark face and tawny eyes beneath straight black brows gleaming with amusement and something infinitely more disturbing.

She banished it. Drew a steadying breath. 'How's the sermon going?'

'All done. But if the caravans have returned, perhaps I should write an alternative on brotherly love, just to be on the safe side.'

He turned to look at her, frowning slightly. 'You look a little pale.'

But at least he didn't mention her wet hair...

She shrugged. 'Too much sun, maybe. I must start wearing a hat.'

'Go and sit down,' he directed. 'And I'll make fresh tea.'

'That would be lovely.' She added demurely, 'And a slice of ginger cake, if you can possibly spare it.'

She arrived at work early the following morning, aware that she hadn't slept too well, for which she blamed the heat.

But she'd awoken feeling rather more relaxed about the incidents of the previous day, apart, of course, from the encounter at the lake. Nothing could reconcile her to that.

She'd even found she was glancing at herself in the mirror as she prepared for bed, imagining that she'd somehow had the chutzpah to walk naked out of the water and reclaim her clothes, treating him contemptuously as if he'd ceased to exist.

After all, she had nothing to be ashamed of. She was probably on the thin side of slender, and her breasts might be on the small side, but they were firm and round, her stomach was flat and her hips nicely curved.

At the same time, she was glad she'd stayed in the lake.

Because the first man to see her nude was going to be Patrick, she thought firmly, and not some insolent, low-life peeping Tom.

As she let herself in through the school's rear entrance, she heard Mrs Wilding's voice raised and emotional, mingling with Patrick's quieter more placatory tones.

He must have told her about us, was her first thought, the second being a cowardly desire to leave before anyone knew she was there. To jump before she was pushed.

'Oh, don't be such a fool,' Mrs Wilding was raging. 'Don't you understand this could finish us? Once word gets out, the parents will be up in arms, and who can blame them?'

A reaction that could hardly be triggered by her relationship with Patrick, Tavy decided.

As she appeared hesitantly in the sitting room doorway, Patrick swung round looking relieved. 'Tavy, make my mother some tea, will you? She's—rather upset.'

'Upset?' Mrs Wilding repeated. 'What else do you expect? Who in their right mind would want their innocent, impressionable child to be exposed to the influence of a drug-addled degenerate?'

Tavy, head reeling, escaped to the kitchen to boil the kettle, and measure Earl Grey into Mrs Wilding's favourite teapot with the bamboo handle. This was clearly an emergency and the everyday builder's blend would not do.

'What's happened?' she whispered when Patrick arrived for the tray.

'I ran into Chris Abbot last night, and we went for a drink. He was celebrating big time.' Patrick drew a deep breath. 'Believe it or not, he's actually sold the Manor at last.'

'But that's good, surely.' Tavy filled the teapot. She found one of her employer's special porcelain cups and saucers, and the silver strainer. 'It needs to be occupied before thieves start stripping it.'

Patrick shook his head. 'Not when the buyer is Jago Marsh.'

He saw her look of bewilderment and sighed. 'God, Tavy, even you must have heard of him. Multimillionaire rock star. Lead guitarist with Descent until they split up after some monumental row.'

Something stirred in her memory, left over from her brief time at university. A group of girls on her landing talking about a gig they'd been to, discussing with explicit detail the sexual attraction of the various band members.

One of them saying, 'Jago Marsh—I have an orgasm just thinking about him.'

Suppressing an instinctive quiver of distaste, she said slowly, 'Why on earth would someone like that want to live in a backwater like this?'

He shrugged, then picked up the tray. 'Maybe backwaters are the new big thing, and everyone wants some.

'According to Chris, he was at a party in Spain and met Sir George's cousin moaning he had a country pile he couldn't sell, no reasonable offer refused.'

'He's changed his tune.' Tavy followed him down the passage to the sitting room.

'Seriously strapped for cash, according to Chris. So Jago Marsh came down a while back, liked what he saw, and did the deal.' He sighed. 'And we have to live with it.'

Mrs Wilding was sitting in a corner of the sofa, tearing a tissue to shreds between her fingers. She said, 'I would have bought the place myself when it first came on the market. After all, I've been looking to expand for some time, but my offer was turned down flat. And now it's gone for a song.'

'But still more than you could afford,' Patrick pointed out.

'There were other offers,' his mother said. 'Why doesn't Christopher Abbot check to see if any of them are still interested? That way the Manor could be sold for some decent purpose. Something that might bring credit to the area.'

'I think contracts have already been exchanged.'

'Oh, I can't bear to think about it.' Mrs Wilding took the tea that Tavy had poured for her. 'This man Marsh is the last type of person we want living here. He'll destroy the village. We'll have the tabloid newspapers setting up camp here. Disgusting parties keeping us all awake. The police around all the time investigating drugs and vice.' She shook her head. 'Our livelihood will be ruined.'

She turned to Tavy. 'What is your father going to do about this?'

Tavy was taken aback. 'Well, he certainly can't stop the sale. And I don't think he'd want to make any pre-judgements,' she added carefully.

Mrs Wilding snorted. 'In other words, he won't lift a finger to protect moral standards. Whatever happened to the Church Militant?'

She put down her cup. 'Anyway, it's time you made a start, Octavia.

'You'll find yesterday's correspondence waiting on your desk. When you've dealt with that, Matron needs a hand in the linen room. Also we need a new vegetable supplier, so you can start ringing round, asking for quotes.'

From doom and disaster to business as usual, thought Tavy as she went to her office. But to be fair, Mrs Wilding probably had every right to be concerned now that this bombshell had exploded more or less on her doorstep.

She found herself wondering if the unpleasant tough at the lake was the shape of things to come. Security perhaps, she thought. And I rambled on about CCTV. No wonder he was amused.

Let's hope he advises his boss to increase the height of the perimeter wall, and then they both stay well behind it.

It was a busy morning, and Mrs Wilding's temper was not improved when Tavy gave her the list of bedding, towels and table linen that Matron considered should be replaced as a matter of urgency before the start of the new school year in September, and told her that no one seemed able to provide vegetables more cheaply or of a better quality than the present supplier.

'Perhaps I should wait and see if we still have any pupils by the autumn,' Mrs Wilding said tight-lipped, and told Tavy she could go.

Tavy's own spirits had not been lightened by Patrick whispering apologetically that he wouldn't be able to see her that evening after all.

'Mother wants a strategy meeting over dinner, and under the circumstances, I could hardly refuse.' He gave her a swift kiss, one eye on the door. 'I'll call you tomorrow.'

As she cycled home, Tavy reflected that for once she was wholly on the side of her employer. Because the advent of Jago Marsh could well be the worst thing to hit the village since the Black Death, and, even if he didn't stay for very long, the damage would probably be done and quiet, sleepy Hazelton Magna would never be the same again.

Pity he didn't stay in Spain, she thought, as she parked her bike at the back of the house and walked into the kitchen.

Where she stopped abruptly, her green eyes widening in horror as she saw who was sitting at the scrubbed pine table with her father, and now rising politely to greet her.

'Ah, here you are, darling,' the Vicar said fondly. 'As you can see, a new neighbour, Jago Marsh, has very kindly come to introduce himself.

'Jago—this is my daughter Octavia.'

'Miss Denison.' That smile again, but faintly loaded. Even—oh, God—conspiratorial. One dark brow quirking above that mocking tawny gaze. 'This is indeed a pleasure.'

Oh, no, she thought as a wave of hotly embarrassed colour swept over her. It's the Dark Lord himself. I can't—I don't believe it…

Only this time he wasn't in black. Today it was blue denim pants, and a white shirt, unbuttoned at the throat, with its sleeves rolled back to his elbows, adding further emphasis to his tan. That unruly mass of dark hair had been combed back, and he was clean-shaven.

He took a step towards her, clearly expecting to shake hands, but Tavy kept her fists clenched at her sides, tension quivering through her like an electric charge.

'How do you do,' she said, her voice on the chilly side of neutral, as she observed with astonishment a couple of empty beer bottles and two used glasses on the table.

'Jago is a musician,' Mr Denison went on. 'He's coming to live at the Manor.'

'So I've heard.' She picked up the dirty glasses and carried them to the sink. Rinsed out the bottles and added them to the recycling box.

Mr Denison looked at his guest with a faint grimace. 'Ah,' he said. 'The village grapevine, I'm afraid.'

Jago Marsh's smile widened. 'I wouldn't have it any other way. As long as they keep their facts straight, of course.'

'Don't worry,' Tavy said shortly. 'They generally get the measure of newcomers pretty quickly.'

'Well,' he said. 'That can work both ways. And, for the record, I'm now a retired musician.'

'Really?' Her brows lifted. 'After the world arenas and the screaming fans, won't you find Hazelton Magna terribly boring?'

'On the contrary,' he returned. 'I'm sure it has many hidden charms, and I'm looking forward to exploring all of them.' He allowed an instant for that to register, then continued, 'Besides, I've been looking for somewhere quiet—to settle down and pursue other interests, as the saying goes. And the Manor seems the perfect place.'

He turned to the Vicar. 'Particularly when I found a beautiful water nymph waiting for me at the lake. A most unexpected delight and what irresistibly clinched the deal for me.'

Tavy reached for a cloth and wiped out the sink as if her life depended on it.

'Ah, the statue,' Mr Denison mused. 'Yes, it's a lovely piece of sculpture. A true classic. One of the Manning ancestors brought her home from the Grand Tour back in the eighteenth century. Apparently he was so pleased with his find that he even renamed the house Ladysmere for her. Until then it had just been Hazelton Manor.'

'That's a great story,' Jago Marsh said, thoughtfully. 'And I feel exactly the same about my alluring nymph, so Ladysmere it shall stay. I wouldn't dream of changing it back again.'

'But the house itself,' Tavy said very clearly. 'It's been empty for so long, won't it cost a fortune to put right? Are you sure it's worth it?'

'Octavia.' Her father sounded a note of reproof. 'That's none of our business.'

'Actually, it's a valid question,' said Jago Marsh. 'But I'm in this for the long haul, and I like the quirkiness of the place, so I'll pay what it takes to put it right. Although I suspect what it most needs is TLC. Tender loving care,' he added, surveying her flushed and mutinous face, before allowing his gaze to travel down over the white blouse and dark grey skirt worn well below the knee, according to Mrs Wilding's dictates.

'Thank you,' she said. 'I am familiar with the expression.'

How dared he do this? she raged inwardly. How dared he come here and wind her up? Because that's all it was.

Maybe he was just piqued that she hadn't recognised him yesterday. Maybe he'd thought one glance, a gasp and a giggle as realisation dawned, would bring her out of the water and…

Well, she didn't want to contemplate the rest of that scenario.

And with a lot of girls, he might have got lucky, but she had no interest in rock music, or the people who played it, so she was no one's idea of a groupie.

As well as being spoken for, she added swiftly.

Although, it would have made no difference if she'd been free as air. However famous, however rich he might be, she had known him instantly as someone to be avoided. Someone dangerous with a streak of inner darkness.

His talk of settling down was nonsense. She'd give him three months of village life before he was looking for the shortest route back to the fast lane.

Well, she could survive that long. It was enduring the rest of this visit which would prove tricky.

Oh, let it be over soon, she whispered inwardly, and with unwonted vehemence.

But her father was speaking, driving another nail into her coffin. 'I've asked Jago to stay for lunch, darling. I hope that's all right.'

'It's cold chicken and salad,' she said tautly, groaning silently. 'I'm not sure there's enough to go round.'

'But I thought we were having macaroni cheese,' he said. 'I saw it in the fridge when I got the beer.'

And so there was. One of Dad's all-time Saturday favourites. She'd got up specially to prepare it in advance.

'I'd planned that for supper,' she lied.

'Oh.' He looked faintly puzzled. 'I thought you'd be seeing Patrick tonight.'

'Well, no,' she said. 'His mother's had some bad news, so he's spending the evening with her.'

'Ah,' he said, and paused. 'All the same, let's have the macaroni now. It won't take long to cook.'

'Dad.' She tried to laugh. 'I'm sure Mr Marsh can do better for himself than very ordinary pasta in our kitchen.'

'Better than a home-cooked meal in good company?' her antagonist queried softly. 'It sounds wonderful. As long as it isn't too much trouble,' he added, courteously.

Tavy remembered an old Agatha Christie she'd read years ago—*The Murder at the Vicarage*. She felt like creating a real-life sequel.

Hastily, she counted to ten. 'Why don't you both have another beer in the garden,' she forced herself to suggest. 'I—I'll call when it's ready.'

While the oven was heating, she mixed breadcrumbs with Parmesan and scattered them across the top of the pasta, found and opened a jar of plums she'd bottled the previous autumn to have with ice cream as dessert, and made a simple dressing for the salad.

We'll have to eat the chicken tonight, she told herself grimly as she put the earthenware dish into the oven, then turned away to lay the table.

All the domestic stuff she could do on autopilot, which was just as well when her mind seemed to have gone into free fall.

Under normal circumstances, she'd have run upstairs to take off what she regarded without pleasure as her 'school uniform', change into shorts and maybe a sun-top, and release her hair from its clasp at the nape of her neck. Preparation for a lazy afternoon under the chestnut tree in the garden—with a book and the odd bout of weeding thrown in.

But there was nothing usual about today, and it seemed infinitely safer to stay as she was. To show this interloper that the girl he'd surprised yesterday was a fantasy.

And to demonstrate that this was the real Octavia Denison—efficient, hard-working, responsible and mature. The Vicar's daughter and therefore the last person in the world to go swimming naked in someone else's lake.

Except that she had done so, and altering her outer image wasn't going to change a thing as far as he was concerned.

Any more than his lightening of his appearance today had affected her initial impression of him.

She sighed. Her father was a darling but she often wished he was warier with strangers. That he wouldn't go more than halfway to meet them, with no better foundation for his trust than instinct. Something that had let him down more than once in the past.

Well, she would be cautious for him where Jago Marsh was concerned. In fact, constantly on her guard.

She didn't know much about his former band Descent but could recall enough to glean the social niceties had not been a priority with them.

Top of her own agenda, however, would be to find out more, because forewarned would indeed be forearmed.

He's playing some unpleasant game with us, she told herself restively. He has to be, only Dad can't see it.

Although she suspected it was that faith in the basic goodness of human nature that made her father so popular in the parish, even if his adherence to the traditional forms of worship did not always find favour with the hierarchy in the diocese.

But that was quite another problem.

Whereas—sufficient unto the day is the evil thereof, she thought. Which, in this case, was Jago Marsh.

And she sighed again but this time rather more deeply.

CHAPTER THREE

IT WAS ONE of the most difficult lunches she had ever sat through.

And, to her annoyance, the macaroni cheese was one of her best ever, and Jago Marsh praised it lavishly and had two helpings.

To her utter astonishment, her father had gone down to the dark, cobwebby space which was the Vicarage cellar and produced a bottle of light, dry Italian wine which complemented the food perfectly.

She had turned to him, her eyebrows lifting questioningly. 'Should Mr Marsh be drinking if he's driving?'

'Mr Marsh walked from the Manor,' Jago had responded, affably. 'And will return there in the same way.'

Did he mean he'd moved in already? Surely not. The formalities couldn't have been completed. And how could he possibly be living there anyway with no gas, electricity or water and not a stick of furniture in the place?

Somehow she couldn't see him camping there with a sleeping bag and portable stove.

If he'd indeed been the traveller she'd first assumed, she knew now that he'd have had the biggest and best trailer on the site with every mod con and then some.

Just as that cheap metal watch, on covert examination, had proved to be a Rolex, and probably platinum.

What she found most disturbing was how genuinely the

Vicar seemed to enjoy his company, listening with interest to his stories of the band's early touring days, carefully cleaned up, she suspected, for the purpose.

While she served the food and sat, taking the occasional sip of wine, and listening, watching, and waiting.

Let people talk and eventually they will betray themselves. Hadn't she read that somewhere?

But all that their guest seemed to be betraying was charm and self-deprecating humour. Just as if the good opinion of an obscure country clergyman could possibly matter to him.

He's my father, you bastard, and I love him, she addressed Jago silently and fiercely. And if you hurt him, I'll find some way to damage you in return. Even if it takes the rest of my life.

'So, Jago,' the Vicar said thoughtfully. 'An interesting name and a derivative of James I believe.'

Jago nodded. 'My grandmother was Spanish,' he said. 'And she wanted me to be christened Iago, as in Santiago de Compostela, but my parents felt that Shakespeare had knocked that name permanently on the head so they compromised with the English version.'

Iago, thought Tavy, who'd studied *Othello* for her 'A' level English exam. One of literature's most appalling villains. The apparently loyal second in command, turned liar, betrayer and murderer by association. The personification of darkness, if ever there was one.

It felt almost like a warning, and made her even less inclined to trust him.

After the meal, she served coffee in the sitting room. But when she went in with the tray, she found Jago alone, looking at one of the photographs on the mantelpiece.

He said abruptly, not looking round, 'Your mother was very beautiful.'

'Yes,' she said. 'In every way.'

'Your father must be very lonely without her.'

'He's not alone,' she said, defensively. 'He has his work and he has me. Also he plays chess with a retired schoolmaster in the village. And…' She hesitated.

'Yes?'

'And he has God.' She said it reluctantly, expecting some jeering response.

'I'm sure he does,' he said. 'But none of that is what I meant.'

She decided not to pursue that, asking instead, 'Where is he, anyway?' as she set the tray down on the coffee table between the two shabby sofas that flanked the fireplace.

'He went to his study to find a book he's going to lend me on the history of the Manor.'

'The past is safe enough,' she said. 'It's what you may do to its future that worries most people.'

'I met two of my new neighbours on my way here,' he said. 'A man on horseback and a woman with a dog. Both of them smiled and said hello, and the dog didn't bite me, so I wasn't aware of any tsunami of anxiety heading towards me.'

'It may seem amusing to you,' she said. 'But we'll have to live with the inevitable upheaval of your celebrity presence—' she edged the words with distaste '—and deal with the aftermath when you get bored and move on.'

'You haven't been listening, sweetheart.' His tone was crisp. 'The Manor is going to be my home. The only one. And I intend to make it work. Now shall we call a truce before your father comes back? And I take my coffee black without sugar,' he added. 'For future reference.'

'Quite unnecessary,' said Tavy. 'As this will be the first and last time I have to serve it to you.'

'Well,' he said. 'One can always dream.'

Lloyd Denison came striding in, holding a slim book with faded green covers. 'Things are never where you expect them to be,' he said, shaking his head.

That, Tavy thought affectionately, was because he never

put things where they were supposed to go. And she hadn't inherited her mother's knack of guiding him straight to the missing item.

'Thank you.' Jago took the book from him, handling it gently. 'I promise I'll look after it.'

Their coffee drunk, he stood up. 'Now I'll leave you to enjoy your afternoon in peace. But I must thank you again for a delicious lunch. And as home-cooking is currently out of the question for me, I was wondering if you could recommend a good local restaurant.'

'I dine out very rarely, but I'm sure Tavy could suggest somewhere.' Her father turned to her. 'What do you think? There's that French place in Market Tranton.'

Which is our place—Patrick's and mine—thought Tavy, so I'm not sending him there.

She said coolly, 'The pub in the village does food.'

'Yes, but it's very basic,' Mr Denison objected. 'You must know lots of better places.'

She turned reluctantly to Jago. 'In that case, you could try Barkland Grange. It's a hotel and quite a trek from here, but I believe its dining room won an award recently.'

'It sounds ideal.' That smile again. As if he was reaching out to touch her. 'And as I've ruined your supper plans, maybe I can persuade you to join me there for dinner tonight.' He looked at her father. 'And you, sir, of course.'

'That's very kind,' said the Vicar. 'But I have some finishing touches to put to my sermon, plus a double helping of chicken to enjoy. However I'm sure Tavy would be delighted to accompany you.' He looked at her blandly. 'Wouldn't you, darling?'

Tavy reflected she would rather be roasted over a slow fire. But as it had already been established that, thanks to her would-be host, she had no prior date, she was unable to think of a feasible excuse. Her only alternative was a bald refusal which would be ill-mannered and therefore cause distress to her father. Although she suspected Jago himself would be amused.

Accordingly, she murmured an unwilling acquiescence, and agreed that she could be ready at seven-thirty.

Unless mown down in the meantime by a runaway steam-roller. And if she knew where one was operating, she'd lie down in front of it.

As she stood by her father, her smile nailed on, to wave goodbye to the departing visitor, she wondered how close she was to the world record for the number of things that could go wrong within a set time.

Because her choice of Barkland Grange, astronomically expensive and practically in the next county, had rebounded on her big time.

Safely indoors, she rounded on her father. 'Dad, how could you? You practically offered me to him on a plate.'

'Hardly, my dear. He only invited me out of politeness, you know.

'I gather from something he said in the garden, he feels that the pair of you have somehow got off on the wrong foot, and he wants to make amends.' He added gently, 'And I must admit, Tavy, that I did sense something of an atmosphere.'

'Really?' she said. 'I can't think why.' She was silent for a moment, then burst out, 'Oh, Dad, I don't want to have dinner with him. He's out of our league, in some unknown stratosphere, and it worries me.'

And the worst of it is I can't tell you the real reason why I don't want to be with him. Why I don't even want to think about him. Because you'd think quite rightly that I'd been stupid and reckless and be disappointed in me.

She swallowed. 'Why did he come here today?'

'To make himself known as the new resident of the Manor, and my parishioner,' he returned patiently.

'You think it's really that simple?' She shook her head.

'I bet you won't find him in the congregation very often. Also, you seem to have forgotten I'm going out with Patrick.'

'But not this evening, it seems. And Jago, after all, is a stranger in our midst. Will it really hurt so much to keep him company? For all his fame and money, he might be lonely.'

Which is what he said about you...

'I doubt that very much,' she said tautly. 'I'm sure he has a little black book the size of a telephone directory.'

'Perhaps he hasn't unpacked it yet,' her father said gently

Tavy, desperate, delivered the killer blow. 'And I've got nothing to wear. Not for a place like that, anyway.'

'Oh, my dear child,' he said. 'If that's the problem...'

He went into his study, emerging a few minutes later with a small roll of banknotes, which he pushed into her hand. 'Didn't you tell me that a new dress shop had opened in Market Tranton, in that little street behind the War Memorial.'

'Dad.' Tavy gazed down at the money, aghast. 'There's a hundred and fifty pounds here. I can't take all this.'

'You can and you will,' he said firmly. 'I know full well you get paid a pittance for all the hours you put in at that school,' adding drily, 'but presumably you feel it's worth it. And I have a feeling that you'll soon be needing a dress for special occasions.'

Such as an engagement party, Tavy thought with sudden buoyancy, as she grabbed the car keys from their hook. Now that would be worth dressing up for.

While tonight could be endured then forgotten.

As seven-thirty approached, Tavy felt the tension inside her begin to build. She sat, trying to interest herself in the local paper, finding instead she was imagining the following week's edition by which time the news about Jago would have become public knowledge.

And she could only hope and pray that none of the stories printed about him would involve herself.

In the end, she'd bought two dresses, neither as expensive as she'd feared, and both sleeveless with scooped necks, and skirts much shorter than she was accustomed to—one covered in tiny ivory flowers on an indigo background, and the other, which she was wearing that evening, in a wonderful shade of jade green.

She'd chosen this because, among the few pieces of jewellery her mother had left, were a pair of carved jade drop earrings which she'd never worn before, but hoped would give her some much needed confidence.

And for once, her newly washed and shining hair had allowed itself to be piled up on top of her head without too much protest, even if it had taken twice the usual number of pins to secure it there.

She'd even treated herself to a new lipstick in an unusual shade between rust and brown that she found became her far more than the rather soft pinks she normally chose. And was almost tempted to wipe it off, and revert to the dull and familiar. Yet didn't.

Any more than she'd gone into Dad's study and said, 'I have to tell you what happened yesterday…'

Tonight at some point, she would offer Jago Marsh a stiff, well-rehearsed apology for trespassing on his property, then ask if the entire incident could be forgotten, or at least never referred to again. And somehow make it clear that what he'd referred to as 'gentle teasing' was totally unacceptable. As were softly loaded remarks about water nymphs.

After that, if the way she was feeling now was any indication, she might well be sick all over the tablecloth.

She had the cash left over from her shopping expedition tucked into her bag, in case she needed to make a speedy exit by taxi at some point. Her mother, she remembered with a soft catch of the breath, had been a firm believer in what she called 'escape money'.

And how strange she should be thinking in these terms

when millions of girls all over the world would give everything they possessed to be in her shoes this evening. And so they could be, she thought, grimacing. She was wearing her only decent pair of sandals and they pinched.

When the doorbell rang, she felt her heart thud so violently that she almost cried out.

I shouldn't have dressed for the restaurant, she thought, as she made her way into the hall. I should be wearing a T-shirt and an old skirt—maybe the denim one I've had since school. Something that would make him wish he'd never put me on the spot—never asked me, as well as ensuring that he won't do it again.

Her father was ahead of her, opening the front door, smiling and saying she was quite ready. Then, to her embarrassment, telling her quite seriously that she looked beautiful, and wishing her a wonderful evening.

So she was blushing and looking down at the floor, only realising at the last moment that the man waiting for her on the doorstep was not Jago Marsh, but someone much older, grey haired and wearing a neat, dark suit.

'Evening, Miss Denison.' A London accent. 'I'm Charlie, Mr Jago's driver. Can you get down the drive in those heels, or shall I fetch the car up?'

'No.' Her flush deepened. 'I—I'm fine.' *If a little bewildered...*

Her confusion deepened when she realised that she would be travelling to Barkland Grange in solitary state.

'The boss had a load of emails to deal with,' Charlie told her. 'Last-minute stuff. Or he'd have come for you himself. He sends his apologies.'

'Oh, that's all right,' Tavy muttered as she was helped into the big grey limousine with tinted windows. In fact, she added silently, it was all to the good. At least she'd be spared his company for a while.

Charlie was solicitous to her comfort, asking if the car

was too hot or too cold. Whether or not she'd like to listen to the radio.

She said again that she was fine, wondering what he'd do if she said that she'd really like to go home, so could he please turn the car around.

But of course she wasn't going to say that because this was her own mess, and it wouldn't be fair to involve him or anyone else.

One evening, she thought. That was all she had to get through. Then, her duty done, she could tell her father with perfect truth that she and Jago Marsh were chalk and cheese, and tonight would never be repeated.

Besides there was Patrick to consider. Patrick whom she could and should have been with tonight.

It's time we talked seriously, she thought. Time we got our relationship on a firm footing and out in the open, for everyone to see, particularly his mother. Made some real plans for the future. Our future.

And she found herself wondering, as the limo smoothly ate away the miles between Hazelton Magna and Barkland Grange, why, when she'd been quite content to let matters drift, this change should now seem to be of such pressing and paramount importance.

And could not find a satisfactory answer.

Her first sight of Barkland Grange, a redbrick Georgian mansion set in its own sculptured parkland, with even a small herd of deer browsing under the trees, seemed to confirm everything she'd heard about it and more.

She sat rigidly, staring through the car window, feeling her stomach churn with renewed nerves. Cursing herself for not having found an excuse—any excuse—to remain safely at home, sharing the cold chicken and later a game of cribbage with Dad.

She could only hope now that Jago's email correspondence had been more involved than expected.

Because if he's not here, she thought, I'd be perfectly justified in saying that I'm not prepared to hang around waiting for him to show up. And if Charlie won't drive me back, I'll simply use my escape money.

And then she saw the dark figure standing on the stone steps in front of the main entrance and knew, with a sense of fatalism, that there was no way out.

'So you have come after all.' She heard that loathsome note of amusement under his drawl, as he opened the car door. 'I was afraid that a migraine, or a sudden chill brought on by unwise bathing might have prevented you.'

'And I was afraid you'd make me produce a doctor's note,' she said, lifting her chin as she walked beside him into the hotel, hotly aware of the candid appraisal that had swept her from head to toe as she emerged from the car.

Resentful too of the light guidance of his hand on her arm—the first time, she realised, that he'd touched her—but reluctant to pull away under the benevolent gaze of the commissionaire holding the door open for them.

He took her across the spacious foyer to a bar, all subdued lighting and small comfortable armchairs grouped round tables, most of which were occupied.

'It's very busy,' Tavy said, praying inwardly that the Grange was too expensive and too distant from Hazelton Magna to attract anyone who might recognise her.

'Weekends here are always popular, I'm told,' Jago returned as a waiter appeared and conducted them to an empty table tucked away in a corner. 'I considered ordering dinner in my suite, but I decided you'd probably feel safer in the dining room. At least on a first date.'

Tavy, sinking back against luxurious cushions, sat upright with a jolt. On several counts.

'Suite?' she echoed. 'You have a suite here?'

'Why, yes.' He was leaning back, supremely at ease in his dark charcoal suit and pearl grey collarless shirt. 'I've been here on and off for several weeks. I thought it would be easier to deal with the purchase of the Manor from a local base, and this proved ideal.' He smiled at her. 'And you were quite right about the food,' he added lightly.

'You knew all about it already—and you didn't say. You let me ramble on…'

'Hardly that. You were quite crisp on the subject. And I was impressed. I'd anticipated being directed to the nearest greasy spoon.

'And as you'd suggested eating here, I couldn't be suspected of any ulterior motive. Better and better.' He nodded to the still-hovering waiter. 'I've ordered champagne cocktails,' he added. 'I hope you like them.'

She said in a small choked voice, 'You know perfectly well I've never had such a thing in my life.'

'Then I'm glad to be making the introduction.'

'And this is not a first date!'

The dark brows lifted. 'You feel we've met before—in a previous existence, maybe? Wow, this is fascinating.'

'I mean nothing of the kind, and you know that too.' She drew a shaky breath. 'I'm here because I didn't have a choice. For some reason, you've made my father think you're one of the good guys. I don't share his opinion. And I'd like to know how the hell you came to be sitting in our kitchen anyway.'

'That's easy,' he said. 'I'd invited Ted Jackson up to the Manor this morning to give me a quote on clearing the grounds. As he was leaving, I simply asked him the identity of the gorgeous redhead I'd seen around. I admit his reply came as something of a surprise, so I decided to pursue my own enquiries.'

The drinks arrived, and he initialled the bill, casually adding a tip, while Tavy stared at him, stunned.

'You—asked Ted Jackson?' she managed at last.

'Yes,' he said. 'I want to use local labour for the renovations as far as possible. Why? Isn't he any good?'

'Yes—I think… How would I know?' She swallowed. 'I mean—you actually asked him about me.'

'It's a useful way of gaining information.'

'He will tell his wife that you did,' she said stonily. 'And June Jackson is the biggest gossip in a fifty-mile radius.' Although she doesn't seem to know I'm seeing Patrick, she amended swiftly. So she's not infallible.

He shrugged. 'You may be right, but he seemed to be far more interested in the prospect of restoring the gardens to their former glory.'

'Until she makes him repeat every word you said to him,' Tavy said bitterly. 'Oh, God, this is such a disaster. And if anyone finds out about this evening…' Her voice tailed away helplessly.

'Single man has dinner with single woman,' he said. 'Sensational stuff.'

'It isn't funny.' She glared at him.

'Nor is it tragic, sweetheart, so lighten up.' He glanced round. 'I don't see any lurking paparazzi, do you?'

'You think it won't happen? That the press won't be interested in notorious rock star suddenly turning village squire?'

'I like the sound of that,' he said. 'Maybe I should grow a moustache that I can twirl.'

'And perhaps you could give up the whole idea,' she said passionately. 'Put the place back on the market, so it can be sold to someone who'll contribute something valuable to the community, instead of causing it untold harm to satisfy some sudden whim about being a landowner, then walking away when he gets bored.'

She paused, 'Which I suppose was what happened with Descent.'

'No,' he said. 'Not exactly.' He picked up his glass. Touched it to hers. 'But here's to sudden whims.' Adding ironically, 'Especially when they come at the end of a long and fairly detailed property search. Because I'm staying, sweetheart, so you and the rest of the neighbourhood will just have to make the best of it.'

He watched her fingers tighten round the stem of her own glass. 'And if you're planning to throw that over me, I'd better warn you that I shall reciprocate, causing exactly the kind of furore you seem anxious to avoid.

'It's up to you, of course, but why not try some and see that it's too good to waste on meaningless gestures.'

She relinquished the glass, and reached for her bag. 'On the whole, I'd prefer to go home.'

'Then I shall follow you,' he said silkily. 'Begging, possibly on my knees, for very public forgiveness of some very private sin. How about, "Come back to me, darling, if only for the sake of the baby." That should get tongues wagging.'

Tavy stared at him, assimilating the faint smile that did not reach his eyes, and unwillingly subsided, deciding she could not take the risk.

'Very wise,' he said. 'Now, shall we begin the evening again? Thank you so much for giving me your company, Miss Denison. You look very lovely, and I must be the envy of every man in the room.'

The tawny gaze held hers, making it somehow impossible to look away. She said shakily, 'Do you really think that's what I want to hear from you?'

'No,' he said, with sudden curtness. 'So let's discuss the menus they're bringing over to us instead. And please don't tell me you couldn't eat a thing, because I noticed you only picked at your lunch. And the chef has an award. You told me so yourself.'

'Tell me something,' she said, her voice barely above a whisper. 'Why are you doing this?'

His smile was genuine this time, and, in some incredible way, even disarming.

'A sudden whim,' he said. 'That I found quite irresistible. It happens sometimes.'

He added more briskly, 'And now that I've satisfied your curiosity, let's see what we can do for your appetite. Why don't we begin with scallops?'

CHAPTER FOUR

THE SCALLOPS WERE superb, grilled and served with a little pool of lobster sauce. The lamb cutlets that followed were pink and delicious, accompanied by rosti and some wonderfully garlicky green beans. The dessert was a magically rich chocolate mousse.

As Jago remarked, simple enough food but exquisitely done.

'Rather like your macaroni cheese,' he added, and grinned at her.

Making it incredibly difficult not to smile back. But not impossible, she found, taking another sip of the wine poured almost reverently into her glass by the *sommelier*. That is, if you were sufficiently determined not to be charmed, enticed and won over. Because that seemed to be his plan.

However, she couldn't deny that the ambience of the place was getting to her. The immaculate linen and crystal on the tables. The gleaming chandeliers. The hushed voices and occasional soft laughter from the other diners. And, of course, the expert and deferential waiters, who were treating her like a princess even though she must have been wearing the cheapest dress in the room.

While her companion was certainly the only man present not observing the dress code.

'I bet you're the only person in the country allowed in here without a tie,' Tavy said, putting down her spoon and suppressing a sigh of repletion. 'Don't you ever worry that people will refuse to serve you? Or is your presence considered such an accolade that they overlook minor details like house rules?'

'The answer to both questions is no,' he said, and frowned. 'And I think I had a tie once. I'll have to see if I can find it. As it matters so much to you.'

'Nothing of the kind,' Tavy said quickly. 'It was just a remark.'

'On the contrary,' he said, leaning back in his chair. 'I see it as a great leap forward. Now it's my turn.' He paused. 'I read some of your father's book this afternoon. The Manor seems to have had a pretty chequered history, hacked about by succeeding generations.'

'I believe so.'

'But it's in safe hands now.' As her lips tightened, he added quietly, 'I wish you'd believe that, Octavia.'

'It's really none of my concern,' she said stiffly. 'And I had no right to speak as I did earlier. I—I'm sorry.' *And you have no right to call me Octavia...*

'But you still wish you hadn't been cornered into coming here tonight.'

'Well—naturally.'

'Because you'd hoped you'd never set eyes on me again.'

She flushed. 'That too.'

'And you'd like very much for us both to forget our first encounter ever happened.'

'Yes,' she said. 'Yes, I would.'

'Very understandable. And for me, anyway, quite impossible. The vision of you rising like Venus from the waves will always be a treasured memory.' He paused. 'And I like your hair loose.'

She was burning all over now. It wasn't just what he'd said, but the way he'd looked at her across the table, as if her dress—her underwear—had ceased to exist under his gaze. As if her hair tumbling around her shoulders was her only covering. And as if he knew that her nipples in some damnable way were hardening into aching peaks inside the lacy confines of her bra.

But if her skin was fire, her voice was ice. 'Fortunately, your preferences are immaterial to me.'

'At present anyway.' He signalled to a waiter. 'Would you like to have coffee here or in the drawing room?'

She bit her lip. 'Here, perhaps. Wherever we go, there'll be people staring at you. Watching every move you make.'

'Waiting for me to start breaking the place up, I suppose. They'll be sadly disappointed. Besides, I'm not the only one attracting attention. There's a trio on the other side of the room who can't take their eyes off you.'

She glanced round and stiffened, her lips parting in a gasp of sheer incredulity.

Patrick, she thought. And his mother. With Fiona Culham, of all people. But it isn't—it *can't* be possible. He couldn't possibly afford these prices—I've heard him say so. And Mrs Wilding simply wouldn't pay them. So what on earth is going on? And why is Fiona with them?

As her astonished gaze met theirs, they all turned away, and began to talk. And no prizes for guessing the main topic of conversation, Tavy thought grimly.

'Friends of yours?'

'My employer,' she said briefly. 'Her son. A neighbour's daughter.'

'They seem in no hurry to come over,' he commented. 'They've been here for over half an hour.'

'I see.' Her voice sounded hollow. 'It looks as if I could well find myself out of a job on Monday.'

His brows lifted. 'Why?'

'I think it's called fraternising with the enemy,' she said tautly. 'Because that's how the local people regard you.'

'Some perhaps,' he said. 'But not all. Ted Jackson, for one, thinks I'm God's gift to landscape gardening.'

'I'm sure you'll find that comforting.' She reached for her bag. 'I think I won't have coffee, after all. I'd like to leave, please, if reception will get me a taxi.'

'No need. Charlie is standing by to take you home.'

She said quickly, 'I'd rather make my own arrangements.'

'Even if I tell you I have work to do, and I won't be coming with you?' There was overt mockery in his voice.

Her hesitation was fatal, and he nodded as if she'd spoken, producing his mobile phone from his pocket.

'Charlie, Miss Denison is ready to go.'

She walked beside him, blisteringly aware of the looks following her as they left the dining room and crossed the foyer. The car was already outside, with Charlie holding open the rear passenger door.

She paused, shivering a little as a sudden cool breeze caught her. She glanced up at the sky and saw ragged clouds hurrying, suggesting the weather was about to change. Like everything else.

She turned reluctantly to the silent man at her side, fixing her gaze on one of the pearl buttons that fastened his shirt. Drew a breath.

'That was an amazing meal,' she said politely. 'Thank you.'

'I suspect the pleasure was all mine,' he said. 'But it won't always be that way, Octavia.'

She could have sworn he hadn't moved, yet suddenly he seemed altogether too close, not even a hand's breadth dividing them. She was burningly aware of the scent of his skin, enhanced by the warm musky fragrance he was wearing. She wanted to step back, but she was rooted to the spot, looking up into the narrow dark face, marking the intensity of his gaze and the firm line of his thin lips.

Wondering—dreading—what he might do next.

He said softly, 'No, my sweet, I'm not going to kiss you. That's a delight I shall defer until you're in a more receptive mood.'

She said in a voice she hardly recognised, 'Then you'll wait for ever.'

'If that's what it takes,' he said. 'I will.' He lifted a hand, touched one of the jade drops hanging from her ear. Nothing more, but she felt a quiver of sharp sensation as if his fingers had brushed—cupped—her breast. As if she would know exactly how that might feel. And want it…

He said, 'Goodnight, Octavia.' And left her.

She sat, huddled into the corner of the rear seat, as the car powered its way smoothly back to the village. Beyond the darkened windows, it was still almost light. It was less than a month to midsummer and, as everyone kept saying, the days were drawing out. Becoming longer. Soon to seem endless.

You'll wait for ever…

She shouldn't have said that, she thought shivering. She knew that now. It was too much like a challenge.

Yet all she'd wanted to do was make it clear that whatever game he was playing must end. That from now on she planned to keep her distance, whatever spurious relationship he tried to hatch with her father.

Who was, of course, the next hurdle she had to negotiate. Just as soon as she got home.

Somehow she had to convince the Vicar that the evening had been a dismal failure.

'Great food,' she could say. 'Shame about the company. Because if he's lonely, Dad, I can quite understand why.' Keeping it light, even faintly rueful, but adamant all the same.

And there, hopefully, it would end.

Mrs Wilding, however, might be a totally different matter, she thought, groaning inwardly. The ghastly mischance that had prompted them to choose Barkland Grange tonight matched up with the way her luck was generally going. While Fiona's presence was the cherry on the cake.

So that was something else not to tell Dad—that she might soon be out of work. Which she couldn't afford to be.

Plus the likelihood that the Manor's new owner's query about 'the gorgeous redhead' would soon be all round the village, lighting its own blue touchpaper.

All in all, the tally of her misfortunes seemed to be on an upward spiral since Jago Marsh's arrival.

I hit the nail on the head when I called him the Dark Lord, she thought, biting her lip savagely.

When they got to the Vicarage, Charlie insisted on easing the limo carefully up the narrow drive.

'You don't know who might be lurking in those shrubs, miss,' he informed her darkly. 'I'm dropping you at the door.'

'We don't actually have many lurkers in Hazelton Magna,' she told him, adding silently, 'Apart from your boss.' But she thanked him all the same, and even managed a wave as he drove off.

But when she tried the door, it was locked, and it was then she noticed that the whole house seemed to be in darkness. Perhaps there'd been an emergency—someone seriously ill—and her father had been sent for, as often happened with the older parishioners, and sometimes with the younger ones too.

Or more prosaically, perhaps Mr Denison, not expecting her home so soon, had simply decided to have an early night.

She let herself in quietly, slipped off her sandals and trod upstairs barefoot to investigate, and offer a cup of hot chocolate if her father was still awake.

But his door was open and the bed unoccupied.

Ah, well, a sick visit it is, she decided as she returned downstairs. And quite some time ago, because when she took the milk from the fridge, she noticed the cold chicken was still there under its cling-film cover.

He'll be starving when he comes in, she thought, mentally reviewing the cartons of homemade soup waiting in the freezer, and deciding on minestrone.

But as she went to retrieve it, a key rattled in the back door lock, and Mr Denison came in, not with the withdrawn, strained look he wore after visiting people in trouble, but appearing positively cheerful.

'Hello, darling. Foraging for food? Was the Barkland Grange catering that bad?'

'No, I saw you'd had no supper, so I was getting something for you.'

'Oh, I've been dining out too,' he said. 'Geoff Layton phoned to say his son had sent him a birthday hamper from Fortnum's. So we had chess and the most wonderful pork pie.' He patted his midriff. 'Quite amazing.'

'Oh.' She closed the freezer door. 'How lovely.'

'Anyway,' he said. 'How did your evening go?'

'It went,' Tavy said crisply, pouring milk into a pan and setting it to heat. 'For which I was truly thankful. Jago Marsh and I have absolutely nothing in common, and the less I see of him the better.'

'Ah,' he said thoughtfully. 'So no attraction of opposites in this case.'

'No attraction at all,' Tavy returned, firmly quashing the memory of the way he'd looked at her—that light touch on her earring and their admittedly tumultuous effect. It was stress, she told herself, induced by a truly horrible evening. Nothing more.

She poured the hot milk into their cups, and stirred in the chocolate. The usual bedtime ritual.

Which is how I want things, she thought. The everyday, normal way they were forty-eight hours ago.

And that's what I'm going to get back. Whatever it takes. And no intrusive newcomer is going to stop me.

'I still can't believe it,' said Patrick. 'I thought—I hoped I was seeing things. What the hell did you think you were doing?'

'Having dinner,' Tavy retorted, rolling out pastry as if she was attacking it, which did not bode well for the steak and kidney pie they were having for Sunday lunch. 'But maybe it's a trick question.'

She added, 'If it comes to that, I wasn't expecting to see you.' She paused. 'Or Fiona.'

'Her mother called mine,' he said defensively. 'Said she was feeling a bit down over the divorce. So Mother thought it would be nice for her.'

'Very,' said Tavy, reflecting that during their earlier encounter, Fiona seemed to be firing on all cylinders.

'Besides,' he went on. 'In the old days, she was one of the gang.'

Not any gang that I ever belonged to, thought Tavy.

'Anyway,' he added. 'That's not important. Do you realise that Mother was absolutely furious about last night. And that I've had to do some fast talking to stop her from sacking you.'

Or it might also have occurred to her that she'd get no one else to do everything I do for the money, thought Tavy with sudden cynicism. Thought it, but didn't say it.

'Thank you,' she said. 'But it shouldn't have been necessary. For one thing, she doesn't exercise any jurisdiction over how I spend my time outside school hours. Maybe you should have mentioned that.

'For another, I should have been with you last night, and not him. So why wasn't I, Patrick? When are you going to tell her about us?'

'I was about to,' he said defensively. 'But you've knocked that right on the head. Now, I'll just have to wait until she cools down over this entire Jago Marsh business, and it won't be any time soon, I can tell you.'

He shook his head. 'What on earth does your father have to say about all this?'

'Not a great deal,' she said. 'He doesn't seem to share your low opinion of Mr Marsh.' She added stonily, 'And he was also invited last night, but had—other things to do.'

He sighed. 'Tavy, your father's a great chap—one of the best—but not very streetwise. He could get taken in quite badly over all this.'

The fact that this echoed her own thinking did not improve her temper.

'Thank you for your concern,' she said shortly. 'But I don't think he's going to change very much at this stage. Now, if you'll excuse me, I must get this pie in the oven. Dad will be in at any moment, and he has a christening this afternoon.'

'Tavy,' he said. 'Darling—I don't want us to fall out over this. Jago Marsh simply isn't worth it.'

'I agree.' She banged the oven door. 'Perhaps you could also persuade your mother to that way of thinking, so we can all move on.'

She took carrots from the vegetable rack and began to scrape them to within an inch of their lives.

'But you must realise,' he persisted, 'that it's—well— inappropriate behaviour for you to consort with someone like that.'

'Consort?' she repeated. 'That's a very pompous word. But if you're saying you'd rather I didn't have dinner with him again, then you needn't worry, because I haven't the least intention of doing so. Will that satisfy you? And your mother?'

She added coolly, 'Besides, inappropriate behaviour doesn't enter into it. Jago Marsh just isn't my type.'

'While I've been stupid and tactless and made you cross,'

he said quietly. 'I'm sorry, Tavy. Why don't we draw a line under the whole business and go out for a drink tonight?'

For a moment, she was sorely tempted, even if he had ticked all the boxes he'd mentioned and more.

She tried to smile. 'Can we make it another time? Actually, I've promised myself a quiet night at home after Evensong.'

I feel as if I need it, she thought when she was alone. Which isn't me at all. In fact, I feel as if I'm starting to learn about myself all over again. And I don't like it.

It was clear when she reported for duty on Monday morning that her fall from grace had not been forgiven *or* forgotten.

Mrs Wilding was chilly to the nth degree.

'I have to say, Octavia, that I thought your father would share my concerns about this new addition to the neighbourhood. But I gather he seems prepared to accept him at face value, which in my opinion shows very poor judgement.'

Tavy remembered just in time that Mrs Wilding was a prominent member of the parochial church council, which her father chaired as Vicar, and bit her tongue hard.

Fortunately, she did not have to see very much of her employer who departed mid-morning on some unexplained errand, and returned late in the afternoon, tight-lipped and silent.

As soon as she'd signed her letters, she told Tavy she could go home after she'd taken them to catch the post.

Something's going on, Tavy thought as she cycled to the village. But she's hardly likely to confide in me, especially now.

As she was putting the letters into the mail box, June Jackson emerged from the post office.

'Afternoon, Miss Denison.' She lowered her voice, her smile sly. 'I hear you've got yourself an admirer up at the Manor.'

'Then you know more than I do, Mrs Jackson,' Tavy returned coolly. 'It's extraordinary how these silly stories get about,' she added for good measure.

'Just a story, is it?' The smile hardened. 'But there aren't any others with your shade of hair in the village, not that I can call to mind. And I also hear that he didn't waste any time calling at the Vicarage either.'

Tavy climbed back on her bicycle. 'My father has a lot of visitors, Mrs Jackson. It comes with the territory.'

And imagining that anyone could keep anything quiet in this village was too good to be true, Tavy thought as she pedalled home.

As she walked into the house, she could hear him talking on the phone in his study, sounding tired.

'Yes, I understand. I've been expecting something of the kind.' A pause. 'Tomorrow morning then. Thank you.'

For a moment, she hesitated, tempted to go into the study and ask what was going on.

Instead, she called, 'I'm home,' and went to the kitchen to put the kettle on.

She was pouring the tea when her father appeared, leaning a shoulder wearily against the door frame.

He said, 'Someone's coming from the diocesan surveyor's office to look at the church, and prepare a report.'

'But they did that before, surely. Isn't that why you launched the restoration fund?'

'I gather the surveyor's visit is to check what further deterioration there's been in the stonework of the tower, and to carry out a detailed examination of the roof. Apparently they've heard we have to put buckets in the chancel when it rains.'

'Then that must mean they're going to do the repairs,' Tavy said, handing him a mug of tea. 'Which is great news.'

'Well,' he said. 'We can always hope.' He made an effort

to smile. 'And pray.' He turned away. 'Now, I'd better find the estimates we had last time.'

Tavy felt uneasy as she watched him go. Surely there wasn't too much to worry about. Holy Trinity's congregation might not be huge but it was loyal. And if the response to the original appeal had tapered off, the prospect of restoration work actually beginning might kick-start it all over again.

I'll talk to Patrick about it this evening, she thought. He'd texted her at lunchtime to suggest they met for a drink that evening at the Willow Tree, a fifteenth century pub on the outskirts of Market Tranton that was one of their favourite haunts.

And while she was glad that she was going to see him, because it was an opportunity to put things completely right between them again, it also meant she had to get there under her own steam, also known as the local bus which luckily stopped a few yards from the pub door.

But presumably, after Saturday evening's debacle, Patrick was even more wary about openly picking her up in his car in case his mother got to hear of it.

Oh, damn Jago Marsh, she muttered under her breath, taking an overly hasty slurp of tea and burning her tongue.

After all, if she hadn't been pushed into spending the evening with him, there would have been no trouble with Mrs Wilding and her relationship with Patrick might no longer have to be the best-kept secret in the universe.

To add to her woes, it also looked as if June Jackson had been right about the weather. Raindrops were already spattering the kitchen window, so the other new dress she planned to wear would now have to be covered by her waterproof, and her sandals exchanged for navy loafers. Same old, same old, she thought resignedly.

On the other hand, the price of petrol forbade her from asking Dad if she could borrow the Peugeot. That was one of the economies they had to make, and it was important to do so cheerfully.

Which was why it was going to be poached eggs on toast for the evening meal, as her father had finished off yesterday's steak and kidney pie for lunch, without a word about the pastry, which could easily have been used to mend one of the holes in the church roof.

But as her mother had always said, for pastry you needed a light hand and a tranquil heart. And at the moment, she possessed neither.

And said again, this time aloud and with feeling, 'Oh, damn Jago Marsh.'

CHAPTER FIVE

THE PUB WAS busy when Tavy walked in, but she immediately spotted Patrick standing at the bar, and slipped off her raincoat to display the full charm of the indigo dress as she went, smiling, to join him.

'What a hell of a day,' was his greeting. 'I've got you a Chardonnay. Hope that's all right.'

'Fine,' she said untruthfully, telling herself he must have forgotten she much preferred Sauvignon Blanc, and faintly piqued because he hadn't noticed the new dress. 'What's been the matter?'

He shrugged. 'Oh, just another bloody Monday, I suppose. Look, those people are going. Grab their table while I get another pint.'

Bad-tempered Mondays seemed to be a family trait, thought Tavy ruefully as she sat down. Something, perhaps, to bear in mind for the future. Or devise some way of omitting Monday altogether and starting the week on Tuesday instead.

When he joined her, she said, 'It seems to have been one of those days all round. The diocesan surveyor is going to take another look at the church. I think my father's worried about it.'

'I'm not surprised.'

Tavy bit her lip. 'I was hoping for some positive thinking,' she said quietly.

'Not much of that around where money's concerned, I'm afraid.' His tone was blunt. 'And Mother's always said Holy Trinity would cost a fortune to put right. It's been neglected for too long.'

'But not by Dad,' she protested. 'The problems started before he came, and he's done his utmost to get the diocese to take action. Your mother must know that.'

'At the moment, she has her own troubles,' he said stiffly. 'As you of all people must be aware.'

Tavy sighed under her breath and took an unenthusiastic sip of her wine. It was clear that getting back on terms with Patrick, currently staring moodily into his beer, wasn't going to be as simple as she'd first hoped. Because she could never explain how the thing with Jago Marsh had begun or why she'd been pressured into accepting his invitation to dinner.

On the whole, it was best to keep quiet and hope that Jago Marsh would do the same, if not for her sake, then out of what appeared to be genuine respect for her father.

She leaned back in her chair, listening to the ebb and flow of conversation around her, the buzz of people letting their hair down after a working day, the squeak of the door as customers came and went, and, underlying it all, the soft throb of music from the digital jukebox.

She began, almost in spite of herself, to feel soothed and waited to feel that special lift of the heart that being with Patrick usually produced.

The door hinges protested again, accompanied by a draught of cold, damp air, and then, as if a switch had suddenly been thrown, there was silence.

She glanced up in surprise, and saw that everyone was looking towards the door, standing on tiptoe, craning their necks, exchanging looks and comments. And knew, in one heart-stopping instant, exactly who the newcomer must be to be so immediately and universally recognised.

He was wearing his signature black—this time jeans and

a T-shirt—smiling and exchanging greetings with people in
the crowd that was parting for him, giving him access to the
bar. Acknowledging the star in their midst.

Fiona Culham walked beside him in a dress the colour
of mulberries, very cool, very chic, very much in command
of the situation. Possibly even revelling in it.

Tavy saw Jago glance round. Felt him fleetingly register
her presence, then, thankfully, move on.

'Oh, God,' Patrick muttered. 'This is all I need.'

But just what I need, Tavy told herself resolutely. Jago
and Fiona, the perfect pairing. So, no repetition of the other
night's nonsense. No waiting, dreading the moment when
I'd see him again, because whatever game he's been playing
is now over, and there'll be no more…anything between us.

So I can quit worrying and get on with my life. Just as
I wanted.

'Hi,' said Fiona. 'I see it's the usual scrum in here tonight.
Mind if we join you?'

There was certainly room enough at the table. Stunned,
Tavy glanced at Patrick, waiting for him to say something.
Make some excuse. Preferably that they were just leaving.

Only to hear him say stiffly, 'Of course, no problem.'

'Thanks.' Fiona sank gracefully down on to the chair
next to him, then laughed as a blast of raw rhythmic frenzy
surged into the room, amid applause. 'Oh, someone's put on
Easy, Easy. How very sweet.'

Her mocking gaze surveyed Tavy's evident bewilderment.
'Poor Octavia. You've no idea what I'm talking about, have
you? This was Descent's first big hit, my pet. Made them
superstars overnight.'

'And what are they now?' Tavy asked coolly, needled by
the other's patronising tone. 'White dwarfs?'

'Well, at least we haven't disappeared into a black hole,'
Jago said silkily as he joined them, seeming to appear once
again from nowhere. 'Much as many people might wish.

But not the landlord, fortunately.' He smiled round the table, the tawny eyes glittering when they rested briefly on Tavy's flushed face, and the spill of auburn hair on her shoulders. 'In fact, he's sending over champagne as a "welcome to the district" offering.'

He took the seat opposite her, stretching out long legs, making her hurriedly draw back her own chair to avoid any risk of contact. And seeing his mouth curl cynically as he registered her hasty movement.

'Free champagne,' Fiona echoed and gave a little trill of laughter. 'Wow.' She put a perfectly manicured hand on Jago's arm. 'I can see it's going to be non-stop party time in future.

'You must have a house-warming—when the Manor's fit for you to move into. Although my father says you'd be better off pulling it down and starting again. After all, it's hardly a listed building.'

'That's one viewpoint certainly,' Jago said courteously. 'But not one I happen to share.' He paused, looking at Patrick. 'And on the subject of friends and neighbours, shouldn't you introduce me?'

'Of course. How totally dreadful of me,' Fiona gushed. 'This is Patrick Wilding who's a fabulous accountant, and whose mother runs the most marvellous girls' preparatory school in the village.'

She added, 'Funnily enough, Octavia has a little job there too, when she's not rushing round the district, of course, doing good works.' She smiled brilliantly, 'So, Patrick, meet Jago Marsh.'

'How do you do?' Jago leaned forward, proffering a hand which Patrick accepted with barely concealed reluctance, muttering an awkward reply.

Which, in the good manners stakes, left Jago leading by a length, thought Tavy, biting her lip as the champagne arrived in an ice bucket, accompanied by four flutes.

As Jago began to fill them, she said, 'I already have a drink, thank you.' Sounding, she realised with vexation, like a prim schoolgirl.

'Which you don't seem to be enjoying particularly,' he said, looking at her untouched glass. He put a gently bubbling flute in front of her. 'Have this instead.'

'Not for me, thanks,' Patrick said shortly. 'I'll stick to beer.'

'But I still hope you'll join me in a toast.' Jago raised his glass. 'To new beginnings,' he said softly. 'And new friends.'

'Oh, yes.' Fiona touched her glass to his. Her smile flashed again. 'Particularly those.'

This time, it was Tavy's turn to mumble something. She managed a fleeting look at Patrick, who was responding to the toast as if his beer had turned to prussic acid.

But the champagne was wonderful, fizzing faintly in her mouth, cool against her throat. She leaned back in her chair listening to the music, thinking that it hardly matched its title. That it wasn't 'easy' at all, with its intense, primitive rhythm, but wrenched and disturbing as if dragged up from some dark and painful place. An assault on the senses.

It wasn't her kind of music at all, she told herself swiftly, but she couldn't deny its almost feral impact.

Fiona was talking to Jago. 'It must make you feel wonderful, hearing this again. Remembering its amazing success.'

He shrugged. 'To be honest, it just seems a very long time ago.'

'But you were headline news,' she persisted. 'Everyone wanted to know about you.'

'Indeed they did,' he said. 'And what the papers couldn't find out, they made up.'

'And the band's name,' Fiona rushed on. 'People said you really meant to be called "Dissent" because you were in rebellion against society, only someone got the spelling wrong on your first contract.' And she giggled.

'I'm afraid the story is wrong.' His voice was quiet, the tawny eyes oddly brooding. 'Pete Hilton, the bass player and I studied Virgil's *Aeneid* at school, and we took our name from Book Six where the oracle says, *"Facilis descensus Averno"*. Easy is the descent into Hell.' He added wryly, 'Before pointing out that very few who get there make it back again.'

He paused. 'However, it failed to mention that sometimes the demons you find there make the return journey with you.'

Tavy stared at him. His voice had been level, even expressionless but there had been something in his words that had lifted all the hair on the back of her neck.

'You learned Latin?' Fiona did not mask her surprise.

'We all did at my school,' he said, and smiled at her. 'Including, of course, your husband, who was in my year.'

Seeing Fiona Culham thoroughly disconcerted didn't happen often, thought Tavy, a bud of illicit pleasure opening within her, but it was worth waiting for.

'Oh,' the other girl said at last. 'You mean my ex-husband, of course.

'I had no idea you were at the same school.'

He said gently, 'And why should you?'

As the music ended in a wave of clapping and stamping from the other customers, he looked across at Tavy. 'So, what did you think of that blast from the past, Miss Denison?'

'Not much, I bet,' Fiona said dismissively. 'Octavia never listens to anything that can't be found in *Hymns Ancient and Modern*.'

'She's a good judge,' Jago said lightly. 'As someone said, why should the devil have all the best tunes?'

'But I didn't think yours was a tune.' Tavy's voice was quiet. 'It was too angry. It made me feel uncomfortable.' She added, 'But I expect that was the intention.'

There was an odd silence, then Patrick said, 'I'm getting myself another pint.' And went.

'You must excuse me too,' said Fiona, brightly. 'I need to powder my nose.'

Leaving Tavy alone at the table with Jago Marsh in a silence which was suddenly almost tangible.

And which he was the first to break. 'So he isn't just the employer's son?'

'No,' she said, slightly breathless, shakily aware that his eyes were travelling slowly over her, lingering shamelessly on the softly rounded curves tantalisingly displayed by the low neckline of the indigo dress, as if the fabric that covered her no longer existed. As if he was remembering exactly how much he'd seen of her at their first meeting. And, judging by his faint smile, enjoying every moment of the memory.

Making her wish almost desperately that she'd worn something less revealing, and tied her hair back instead of leaving it loose.

And that there was something altogether more substantial than a pub table between them.

Fight back, she thought as, in spite of herself, a slow tingle of awareness shivered through her body. Don't let him do this to you.

She lifted her chin. 'We're—involved.'

He nodded reflectively. 'And how does the employer feel about that?'

'That is none of your business!'

'Oh, dear,' he said lightly. 'That bad, eh?'

'Not at all,' she denied swiftly. 'I simply prefer not to discuss it.' *Especially with you...*

His eyes never left her. 'So, exactly how deep is this involvement, or am I not allowed to ask that either?'

Colour rose in her face. 'No you're not.'

'Which totally confirms my suspicions,' he murmured.

'Well, you have no right to suspect anything,' Tavy countered, her flush deepening. 'Or to indulge in any kind of unwarranted speculation about my personal life.'

'Wow, that's serious stuff,' Jago said, grinning at her. 'I shall consider myself rebuked.'

'Now I'll ask you something,' she said. 'What made you choose the Willow Tree of all places tonight?'

'I didn't,' he said. 'In case you think I'm stalking you or something equally sinister. In fact, the former Mrs Latimer suggested it. She and her father came up to the Manor this morning to introduce themselves, and, as they were leaving, I asked her if she'd like to go for a drink.'

He paused. 'You see? My life, unlike yours, is an open book.'

'But one I'd prefer not to read,' she said crisply, seeing with relief that Patrick was returning from the bar, edging gingerly through the crowd with his brimming glass, his face flushed and sullen. 'Just as I'd rather we kept our distance from each other in future.'

'That could be tricky,' he said thoughtfully. 'Hazelton Magna being such a very small village.' He added softly, 'Besides, Octavia, you were the one who came calling first. If you remember.'

She took a gulp of champagne to ease the sudden tightness in her throat.

She said thickly, 'I'm hardly likely to forget.'

His smile seemed to touch her like the stroke of a finger on her skin. 'Then at least we have that in common,' he murmured and rose politely as Fiona also reappeared.

After that, it was downhill all the way. Once the complimentary champagne was gone, Jago, to Fiona's open satisfaction and her own secret dismay, simply ordered another bottle.

She tried to catch Patrick's eye to hint it was time to go, but her signal was ignored and he went off to the bar in his turn to obtain a third, or, she realised, startled, possibly even a fourth pint.

Which meant that he'd be in no fit state to drive, she

thought, taking a covert peep at her watch, and trying to remember the timing of the last bus.

She'd never known him drink as much before. A pint and a half or maybe a couple of glasses of red wine were generally his limit.

I should have talked to him when I first got here, she told herself unhappily. Persuaded him to tell me what was troubling him. Why his day had been so rotten. Now, there's no chance.

Fiona was off again, describing parties she'd been to in London, film premieres, theatre opening nights. Dropping celebrity names in an obvious effort to establish mutual acquaintances, but without any marked success.

Jago listened politely, but explained that he had spent most of the time since the band split up travelling abroad, and was therefore out of the loop.

'Oh, but once it's known you're back, all that will change,' Fiona said. 'Besides, there was a piece in one of the papers only a few weeks ago, saying Descent might be getting back together. How marvellous would that be?'

'I read that too,' he said. 'Pure speculation.'

'I know you fell out with Pete Hilton,' she said. 'But surely you could find another bass player.'

'Dozens, probably, if we wanted,' he said, refilling her glass.

'But you heard the reaction to *Easy, Easy* here tonight,' she protested. 'Imagine that repeated a million times over.'

'I don't have to use my imagination.' There was a sudden harshness in his voice. 'We experienced it in real life. Now we've made different choices.'

'That's crap and you know it,' Patrick said belligerently. 'With enough money on the table, you'd be off touring again tomorrow.'

Tavy groaned inwardly. She put her hand on his arm. 'I think it's time we were going.'

'No,' he said. 'I want him to admit it.'

Jago looked down at the table, shrugging slightly. 'Fine,' he said. 'Whatever you say, mate.'

'And I'm not your mate,' Patrick retorted. 'Face it, you're going to need a couple more million in the coffers to make that dump you've bought hab-habitable.' He brought the word out with difficulty.

'Which reminds me,' Fiona broke in hurriedly. 'I have a list of some simply marvellous interior designers—top people—that friends of mine used in London. I'll give it to you.'

'Thanks,' Jago said. 'But I've already decided to use only local firms.'

'Lord Bountiful in person,' Patrick muttered. 'Crumbs from the rich man's table. I hope they remember to touch their forelocks.'

Jago's lips tightened, but he said nothing, just turned in his chair and beckoned, and Tavy saw the landlord Bill Taylor approaching.

'Now then, Mr Wilding.' His voice was polite but firm. 'Let's call it a night, shall we? The wife's phoning for a taxi to take you home, so I'll have your keys, if I may, and you can pick up your car in the morning. I'll put it at the back next to mine, so it'll be quite safe.'

'I can drive,' Patrick said. 'I can drive perfectly well, damn your bloody cheek.'

The older man shook his head. 'Sorry, sir. I can't allow that. If anything should happen—if you were picked up by the police, it would reflect on me and the good name of the pub, letting you leave like this.'

He looked at Tavy. 'And I'll make sure you get back safely too, my dear.'

'I'll be fine,' said Tavy, humiliation settling on her like a clammy hand. 'I can catch the bus.'

'On the contrary,' said Jago. 'I'll be taking Miss Denison

home.' As Tavy's lips parted in instinctive protest, he added softly, 'Not negotiable.'

That was all very well, thought Tavy, her throat tightening, but she knew what Fiona's reaction would be to having her evening spoiled in this way. She could almost feel the daggers piercing her flesh.

But when she ventured a glance at the other girl, she found Fiona was not even looking her way. Instead her eyes were fixed on Patrick who was still hunched, red-faced, in his chair.

She looks—almost triumphant, thought Tavy in total bewilderment. But why?

It was an awkward journey, with Charlie at the wheel, and all of them seated in the rear of the car, Jago in the middle. There was plenty of room, but Tavy found herself trying to edge further away just the same, squashing into the corner, and staring fixedly out of the window at very little, as she tried not to hear what the others were saying.

And she could well have done without that faint trace of musky scent in the air, released by the warmth of his skin and reviving memories of her own that she could have dispensed with too.

While even more disturbing was the imminent risk of his thigh grazing hers.

'Ted Jackson.' Fiona's voice had lifted a disapproving notch. 'I do wish you'd talked to Daddy before hiring him. His wife is the most appalling gossip, but Ted can match her, rumour for rumour. You won't be able to keep anything secret.'

'I doubt I have any secrets left,' said Jago. 'The tabloids did a pretty good dissection of my life and crimes while I was still with the band.'

'They say your quarrel with Pete was over a woman.'

'I'm sure they do,' he said. 'However, I prefer the past

to remain that way and concentrate instead on a blameless future.'

'That sounds terribly dull,' Fiona said with a giggle. 'Everyone needs a few dark corners.'

'Even Octavia here?'

Tavy heard the smile in his voice, and bit her lip hard.

'Oh, no,' said Fiona. 'The Vicar's good girl never puts a foot wrong. An example to us all.'

Her tone made it sound a fate worse than death.

'How very disappointing,' he said lightly. 'Yet people like the Jacksons can be very useful. For a newcomer to the district, anyway. You can find out a hell of a lot quite quickly.'

'Well, on no account hire him to build you a swimming pool. We had endless problems and in the end Daddy had to sack him, and bring in someone else to finish the work.'

'That won't be a problem,' said Jago. 'I have no plans for a pool.'

'But you must have, surely. There's that big disused conservatory at the side of the house. It would be ideal.'

'I have other ideas about that,' he said. 'And when I want to swim, I have a lake.'

'You must be joking,' said Fiona with distaste. 'That's a frightful place, all overgrown and full of weeds. You should have it filled in.'

'On the contrary,' he said. 'I find it has a charm all of its own. And when it's been cleared out, I intend to use it regularly. With its naked goddess for company, of course,' he added reflectively.

Bastard, thought Tavy inexcusably, wondering how many bones she would break if she opened the car door and hurled herself out on to the verge.

On the other hand, there wasn't far to go, and she was bound to be dropped off first, she thought, steeling herself, which would leave Jago and Fiona at liberty for—whatever.

Instead, she realised Charlie was taking the left fork for

Hazelton Parva, and the White Gables stud, and groaned silently.

'You will come in for coffee, won't you,' Fiona asked when they reached the house, adding perfunctorily, 'You too, of course, Octavia.'

Jago shook his head. 'Unfortunately, I have to get back to my hotel. I have early meetings in London tomorrow. I'm sorry.'

'Well, I suppose I must forgive you.' There was a pout in her voice, as Charlie opened her door for her. Jago got out too, walking with her to the front entrance.

Tavy turned her head and her attention to the semi-darkness outside the window again. She did not want to see if Jago Marsh was kissing Fiona Culham goodnight. For one thing, it was none of her business. For another...

She stopped right there, finding to her discomfort that she did not want to consider any alternatives.

Then tensed as she realised he was already back, rejoining her in the car. Her heartbeat quickened as she shrank even further into her corner.

He said, 'Are you all right?'

'Yes,' she said. 'I mean—no. I shouldn't be here. I should have stayed with Patrick.'

There was a silence, then he said drily, 'Your loyalty is commendable, but I doubt whether he'd have been much good to you tonight.'

She said in a suffocated voice, 'I think you're vile.'

'No,' he said. 'Just practical.' He paused. 'Does he often get blasted like that?'

'No,' she said hotly. 'He doesn't. And he only had a few pints. I don't understand it.'

'I think it was rather more than that. He was drinking whisky chasers up at the bar too.'

She gasped. 'I don't believe you.'

'You can always check with the landlord,' he said. 'He

warned me what was going on when I ordered the other bottle of champagne.'

'He warned you? Why?'

'I imagine in order to avoid trouble.'

'Oh, it's too late for that,' she said quickly and bitterly. 'Because you're the real cause of the trouble. It started when you came here. When you decided to buy the Manor.'

She took a swift, trembling breath. 'Mrs Wilding, Patrick's mother, is afraid that her pupils' parents will take them away from the school when word gets out that you've come to live in the village. That people won't want their children exposed to your kind of influence. That there'll be disruption—drunken parties—drugs.'

'You've left out sex,' he said. 'But I'm sure that features prominently on the list of righteous objections to my loathsome presence.'

'Can you wonder?' Tavy hit back.

'No,' he said, with a brief harsh sigh. 'The old maxim "Give a dog a bad name and hang him" has held good for centuries. Why should it be different here—in spite of your father's benign guidance?'

He paused. 'And now I may as well justify your dire opinion of me.'

He moved, reaching for her. Pulling her out of her corner and into his arms in one unhurried, irrefutable movement. Moulding her against his lean body.

The cool, practised mouth brushed hers lightly, even questioningly, then took possession, parting her lips with expert mastery, his tongue flickering against hers in a sensuous and subtle temptation totally outside her experience.

Her hands, instinctively raised to brace themselves against his chest and push him away, were instead trapped helplessly between them, and she could feel the tingling, pervasive warmth of his body against her spread palms, the steady throb of his heartbeat sending her own pulses jangling in a response as scaring as it was unwelcome.

Because she needed to resist him and the treacherous, almost languid wave of heat uncurling deep inside her, and the threat of its unleashed power. And knew she should do it now, as his kiss deepened in intensity and became an urgent demand.

Which was something she had to fight, she recognised, in some dazed corner of her mind, while she still had the will to do so.

Only it was all too late, because he, to her shame, was releasing her first. Putting her firmly away from him. And, as he did so, she realised the car had stopped, and that Charlie was already coming round to open the passenger door for her.

She stumbled out, drawing deep breaths of the cool night air, her sole intention to put the Vicarage's solid front door between herself and her persecutor.

Except he was walking beside her, his hand inflexibly on her arm.

As they reached the porch, he said softly, 'A word of advice, my sweet. When you eventually decide to surrender your virginity, choose a man who's at least sober enough to appreciate you.'

She tore herself free and faced him, eyes blazing, nearly choking on the words. 'You utter bastard. How dare you speak to me like that? Don't you ever bloody touch me—come near me again.'

He tutted reprovingly. 'What language. I hope for your sake that none of the morality brigade are listening.'

She spun on her heel, fumbling in her bag for her key, sensing rather than hearing the departure of the car down the drive. Trying desperately to calm herself before facing her father.

As she closed the door behind her, she called, 'Hi, I'm

home.' But there was no reply and once again there were no lights showing.

It seemed that she had the house to herself. And with that realisation, the tight rein on her emotions snapped, and she burst uncontrollably and noisily into a flood of tears.

CHAPTER SIX

Tavy spent a restless, miserable night, and responded reluctantly to the sound of the alarm the following morning.

Clutching a handful of damp tissues, she'd stared into the darkness trying to make sense of Patrick's extraordinary behaviour, and failing miserably.

But the chief barrier between herself and sleep was her body's unexpected and unwelcome response to Jago Marsh's mouth moving on hers. The warm, heavy throb across her nerve-endings, the stammer of her pulses, and, most shamingly, the swift carnal scald of need between her thighs—all sensations returning to torment her.

Reminding her that—just for a moment—she had not wanted him to stop...

She'd been caught off guard—that was all, she told herself defensively. And she would make damned sure that it never happened again.

When she got to the school, Mrs Wilding was waiting impatiently. 'Oh, there you are, Octavia,' she said as if Tavy was ten minutes late instead of five minutes early. 'I want you to sort out the library this morning. Make sure all the books are catalogued, and shelved properly. List any that need to be replaced and repair any that are slightly worn.' She glanced at her watch. 'I shall be going out.'

Tavy could remember carrying out the self-same operation, fully and thoroughly, at the end of the previous term, but knew better than to say so, merely replying, 'Yes, Mrs Wilding.'

As she'd suspected, the library was in its usual neat order, and there was nothing to add to the list of replacements from the last check. Although she could do something brave and daring like creating a parallel list of books, and suggest that the library should be treated to a mass buying programme.

Some hopes, she thought with self-derision as she returned to her cubbyhole. Mrs Wilding liked the idea of a library because it sent a positive literacy message to the parents, but did not regard it as an investment.

She reprinted the original list, then sat staring at the computer screen, wondering how to occupy herself. Apart from the cheerful sound of Radio Two emanating faintly from Matron's room, the place was silent.

Her hand moved slowly, almost in spite of itself, clicking the mouse to take her online, then keying in 'Descent'.

She drew a breath, noting that the entries about them seemed endless. She scrolled down the page and Jago smiled out at her, sitting on a step, a can of beer in his hand, next to a fair-haired guy with a thin, serious face, both of them stripped to the waist and wearing jeans.

For a moment she felt something stir inside her, soft, almost aching, and clicked hastily on to 'The Making of Descent'. She read that while Pete Hilton, the fair serious one, and Jago had met at public school and started writing songs together, they'd only made contact with the other members of the band, keyboard player and vocalist Tug Austin and drummer Verne Hallam when they'd all subsequently enrolled at the Capital School of Art in London.

They'd started playing gigs at schools and colleges in London, their music becoming increasingly successful, allied with a reputation for drinking and wild behaviour, and leading them to be thrown out of art college at the start of their third year.

At first they'd called themselves Scattergun, and it was only when they'd been offered their first recording contract that they changed their name to Descent, soon scoring their first huge, groundbreaking hit with *Easy, Easy*.

Tavy went on reading about the tours, the sell-out concerts, the awards, all accompanied by a riotous, unbridled lifestyle, fuelled by alcohol and, it was hinted, drugs, that apparently became the stuff of legends. Or horror stories.

There were more pictures too, involving girls. She recognised a lot of them—models, film and TV stars, other musicians. The kind who made the covers of celebrity magazines. But not usually half-dressed, dishevelled and hung-over. And many of them entwined with Jago.

The narrative was punctuated by scraps of Descent's music, raw, raunchy, ferocious, and available with one click.

It was, she thought with shocked disbelief, like discovering there were actually aliens on other planets.

Making her realise just how sheltered her life in Hazelton Magna had been from the overheated world of rock music, reality television and instant celebrity. Making her see why Jago's arrival could well be regarded locally as an unwarranted invasion. How, in spite of her regrettable incursion into his grounds, he was the real trespasser.

She wanted to stop reading, but something made her continue. Some compulsion to know everything, as if that could possibly make her understand the inexplicable.

'Sometimes the demons you find there make the return journey with you...'

His words. And she shivered again.

The band, she read, had broken up three years earlier, citing 'artistic differences'. But they had reunited a year later, with a UK tour planned. But this project had been cancelled following Pete Hilton's sudden departure, caused, it was rumoured, by a fight with Jago Marsh. After which Descent had come to an abrupt end, the other band members dispersing, said the article, 'to pursue other interests'.

Like buying neglected country houses, thought Tavy, returning dispiritedly to the computer's home page. And her researches had done nothing to allay her fears or quell her inner disturbance over Jago Marsh. On the contrary, in fact.

Because it was obvious from the tone of the article that, to him, women were merely interchangeable commodities, a series of willing bodies to be enjoyed, then discarded, which was only serving to deepen her resentment of him and the way he'd treated her.

His arrogant assumption that she would enjoy being in his arms.

A 'treat of the week' for the village maiden, no doubt, she thought furiously.

What she needed now was something to take her mind off it all. She required an occupation, and in the absence of any correspondence, she decided to tidy the stationery cupboard, and check whether more letterheads, report forms and prospectuses needed to be ordered.

Demonstrate my efficiency, she thought, pulling a face.

To her surprise, the cupboard was locked, but there was a spare key in Mrs Wilding's desk drawer, eventually locating it under a bulky folder tied up with pink tape which she lifted out and left on top of the desk.

She opened the door, and inspected and rearranged each shelf with methodical care noting down, as she'd suspected, that more uniform lists were needed, plus compliment slips and letterheads. She was kneeling, examining a box of old date stamps that had been pushed to the back of the bottom shelf and forgotten, when an icy voice behind her said, 'What do you think you're doing?'

Tavy turned and saw Mrs Wilding glaring down at her.

'Just checking the supplies.' She got up, feeling faintly bewildered. 'I realised it was some time since I did so.'

'But the cupboard was locked.'

'I got the key from your drawer.'

'Well, in future, kindly do only what you're asked.'

Tavy watched as Mrs Wilding relocked the cupboard, ostentatiously putting the key in her handbag, then replaced the folder in the drawer and slammed it shut.

She said quietly, 'I've made a note of what we need to re-order from the printers, Mrs Wilding. Shall I leave it with the library list?'

'You may as well.' Mrs Wilding paused. 'I shan't need you again today, Octavia. You can go home.'

Faced with an afternoon of freedom at any other time, Tavy would have turned an inner cartwheel. But this felt like being sent away in some kind of disgrace—as if she'd been caught prying—when she was simply doing her job. Because if any of the school's stationery had run out, she knew who'd have been blamed.

She managed a polite, 'Thank you, Mrs Wilding,' then collected her jacket and her bag, and went to find her bicycle.

She was halfway down the drive, when she heard the sound of a powerful engine approaching, and drew in to the verge, just as a big Land Rover came round the corner, with 'White Gables Stud' blazoned on its sides, and Norton Culham at the wheel.

Tavy couldn't remember him ever calling at the school before, so it was truly turning into a day of surprises, although Mr Culham driving past without appearing to notice her was certainly not one of them.

Everything normal there, she thought, giving a mental shrug and continuing on her way. Passing the church, she saw an unfamiliar car parked outside, and remembered the diocesan surveyor was expected.

Damn, she thought. I meant to wish Dad luck.

As she wheeled her bike up the Vicarage drive, she saw there was something in the porch, leaning against the front door, only to realise as she got closer that it was a large florists' bouquet—two dozen crimson roses beautifully wrapped and beribboned.

She picked them up carefully, inhaling their delicate exquisite fragrance, then detached the little envelope from the outer layer of silver-starred cellophane, and took out the card.

There were just two words. 'Peace offering.'

No sender's name, but she knew exactly who needed to make this kind of atonement and whispered, 'Patrick.'

This wonderful, extravagant, *passionate* gesture more than made up for the apologetic phone call that she'd expected but never received.

Smiling, she let herself into the house, and took the flowers through to the kitchen. She'd need at least two if not three vases for them. And wasn't there something about cutting the stems and bruising them in order to prolong the blooming? Because she wanted to keep them fresh not just for days but weeks.

She took out her mobile and, for once, because she wanted to reassure him that peace had indeed broken out, she called him at work.

He answered immediately. 'Tavy?' He sounded surprised and none too pleased. 'What is it? This isn't a good time. I have a client waiting.'

'But you must have known I'd ring,' she said. 'To thank you, and say how truly beautiful they are, and how thrilled I am.'

There was a pause. Then: 'I don't follow you,' he said. 'What's "truly beautiful"? What are you talking about?'

'Your peace offering,' she said, her voice lilting. 'The lovely flowers you just sent me.'

'Flowers?' Patrick's tone was impatient. 'I never sent any flowers. Why would I? It must be a mistake by the florist—

or someone's playing a joke on you. I suggest you get it sorted. Now I really have to go. I'll call you later.'

He disconnected, leaving Tavy standing motionless, clutching the phone, and staring at the bouquet lying on the kitchen table, as if each long-stemmed blossom had suddenly turned into a live snake.

'No,' she said aloud, her voice clipped and harsh in the silence. 'It's not true. They can't be from—*him*. I don't—I won't believe it.'

Peace offering...

She was trembling, her stomach churning in a mix of incredulity, confusion and disappointment. She brought her fist up to her mouth, biting down hard on the knuckle, trying to distract one pain with another.

She'd believed Patrick had sent the flowers because he'd spoiled the previous evening by getting stupidly and aggressively drunk, and she'd expected him to show a measure of remorse. But his attitude on the phone indicated quite clearly that was the last thing on his mind.

She didn't want to speculate what Jago Marsh's motivation might be. She only knew that to receive flowers—and red roses, the symbol of love at that—from someone as cynically amoral as he was, had to be a kind of degradation.

Suggesting to her where they really belonged. She snatched the bouquet from the table and marched out of the house, down the drive to where the bins were awaiting the weekly refuse collection, thrusting the flowers on top of the kitchen waste.

'Good riddance,' she muttered as she went back to the kitchen.

Back in the kitchen, she picked fresh herbs from the pots outside the back door to add to the omelettes she was planning for lunch in case the surveyor joined them, then set about assembling the ingredients for supper's cottage pie.

The browned meat was simmering nicely on the stove with diced onion and carrot when her father returned.

'Well, this is a pleasant surprise,' he said, smiling with an obvious effort.

'I was given the afternoon off.' Tavy saw with concern the bleakness in his eyes.

'Because we have a visitor,' he went on.

So the surveyor was with him, she thought, summoning a welcoming smile. Which froze as Jago Marsh followed him into the kitchen, carrying, she saw with horror, the roses she'd put in the bin only a short while before.

'And also something of a mystery,' her father added. 'We found these beautiful flowers outside, apparently thrown away.'

'I suggested you might be able to shed some light on the subject.' Jago put the bouquet back on the kitchen table, his mouth twisting ironically as he studied her flushed face. 'Can you?'

'Not really,' said Tavy, keeping her voice steady with an effort. 'I—I found them on the doorstep when I got home. They're obviously a mistake.'

'If so, they're an expensive one,' he commented levelly.

'So I—disposed of them,' she added lamely, not looking at him.

'What a shame,' said the Vicar. 'I suppose we should try and trace the recipient, even though the card seems to be missing.'

That, thought Tavy, was because it was currently burning a hole in her pocket.

Aloud, she said, 'Maybe they just weren't wanted. And ours was the nearest bin.'

'Ah,' said her father. 'A token of unrequited love, perhaps. How sad. In which case I'll take them over to the church, where they'll make a welcome change from Mrs Rigby's everlasting spray chrysanthemums.' He lifted the bouquet

carefully from the table. 'Jago came to return the book I lent
him, my dear. See if you can persuade him to stay for lunch.'

He strode purposefully out and a few seconds later Tavy
heard the front door close behind him.

Leaving her alone. With him. In the world's most loaded
silence.

Which he was the first to break. 'So,' he commented sardonically. 'Not peace but a sword?'

She lifted her chin. 'Did you ever doubt it?'

He looked at the mutinous set of her mouth and smiled.
'There were odd moments,' he drawled.

'In your dreams, Mr Marsh,' she said, her breath quicken-
ing. She began to whisk the eggs in an effort to hide that her
hands were trembling. 'And there is no invitation to lunch,'
she threw at him. 'In case you were hoping.'

'I'm not that much of an optimist.' He looked at the bunch
of herbs on the chopping board. 'Besides, you might be
tempted to include hemlock in my share.' He turned to the
door. 'However, please give your father my regards, and tell
him I look forward to our next meeting.'

And there would be one, Tavy thought, as she added the
chopped herbs and seasoning to the eggs. It was almost inevitable. She would simply arrange not to be around when
it happened.

'Has Jago gone?' her father asked on his return, sounding disappointed.

'Unfortunately, yes,' Tavy said with spurious regret. 'He
has places to go, people to see. You know how it is.' She
paused. 'Anyway, how was the meeting?'

'Not good,' Mr Denison said heavily. 'It's bad news, I'm
afraid.'

Tavy abandoned the eggs and made two mugs of strong
tea instead. She sat beside her father at the table and took
his hand. 'I suppose it's the roof.'

'That's certainly part of it. Apparently, it's gone beyond

repair and would need totally replacing.' He paused. 'But the main problem is the tower.'

'So what does he suggest?'

'That we go on as usual until he has given his report to the Bishop and some decision about Holy Trinity's future has been reached.'

He shook his head. 'And, as he pointed out, it's just another church—Victorian Ordinary instead of Victorian Gothic—with no great age or historical significance that might entitle it to special treatment. And, of course, only a small congregation.'

He took a deep breath. 'I suspect the Bishop means to close it.'

'But he can't do that,' Tavy protested. 'It's an important part of village life.'

He shook his head. 'Sadly, darling, it's happened to other churches in the diocese with similar problems.' He sighed. 'And as you know the Bishop is a moderniser, so we haven't always seen eye to eye in the past.'

Tavy swallowed. 'Would we have to leave this house?'

'Almost certainly. It's a valuable piece of real estate—more so than the church itself, I fear.' He added quietly, 'I'll probably be asked to join the team ministry in Market Tranton.'

As Tavy brought the omelettes to the table, she said, 'Dad, we have to fight this closure. Try to raise some serious money to kick-start the restoration fund again.'

'I've been thinking along the same lines,' he said. 'But where would we start?' He shook his head. 'What we really need is a miracle or a millionaire philanthropist, but they're in short supply these days.'

It was a good omelette but, to Tavy, it tasted like untreated leather. Because she could think of someone just about to lavish thousands of pounds on a country mansion—just to feed his own selfish vanity.

To them that hath, she thought bitterly. And it had never seemed more true, or more horribly unfair.

Oh, damn Jago Marsh, and send him back to the hell he came from. And where he truly belongs, with his drink and his drugs. And his frightful bloody women.

'Octavia, my dear,' the Vicar said gently. 'I know we must fight, but for a moment there you looked almost murderous.'

'Did I?' She smiled at him. Kept her voice light. 'Oh, dear. I must have been thinking of the Bishop.'

CHAPTER SEVEN

EVEN WHEN SCHOOL resumed after half term, Tavy appeared to be still in the doghouse over the stationery cupboard incident.

On the face of it, this was the least of her worries. But the children's return kept her busy and stopped her examining too closely the rest of the uneasiness piling up like thunder clouds at the back of her mind. At least in the daytime.

The nights, when sleep was often strangely elusive, were a different matter, leaving her prey to her churning thoughts.

The major worry, naturally, was Holy Trinity and the awaited surveyor's report. Wasn't that what judges did before passing sentence—ask for reports? And was that how her father felt—as if he was a prisoner in some dock, his future being decided by strangers?

He was almost as quiet and preoccupied as he had been after her mother's death, she thought sorrowfully. As if some inner light had gone out.

Four years ago, she'd made a simple choice that she was sure in her heart was the right one. Now suddenly there were no more certainties, and she felt frightened as well as confused.

And Patrick was part of that confusion. Every day she'd expected to hear from him, via a phone call or a text, but there'd been nothing. So she'd called the flat in the evening a couple of times, but found only the answerphone, and had rung off without leaving a message, because she couldn't think of anything to say that wouldn't make her sound needy.

Yet wasn't talking over problems what people in love were supposed to do? Especially when they might affect the future. *Their* future, which now seemed to be a major part of the general uncertainty.

And there were other aspects of the immediate future to trouble her too, with the village grapevine humming with news.

Ted Jackson and his crew had started work on the Ladysmere grounds, as June Jackson importantly informed everyone.

'Even that old greenhouse place at the back is being rebuilt, and special lighting installed,' she'd announced in the Post Office, pursing her lips before adding with heavy significance, 'No need to ask what for.'

Tavy was halfway home before she realised that Mrs Jackson was hinting it would be used to produce cannabis, and wondered if that was what Jago had meant by 'other ideas'.

Wait till Mrs Wilding hears that, she thought groaning inwardly. She'll be on the phone to the Drugs Squad in minutes.

Jago Marsh himself had not been seen in the village all week, but the constant gossip about his plans for Ladysmere possibly explained why, when she did sleep, Tavy's fleeting, disturbing dreams so often seemed to feature a dark-haired, tawny-eyed man.

Proving, she thought bitterly, that 'out of sight' did not necessarily mean 'out of mind'.

It made her head spin to realise that only a month ago, she'd been scarcely aware of his existence, her life set in a peaceful, secure groove, untouched by any hint of sex, drugs or rock 'n' roll.

Now, she was being forced to acknowledge how swiftly and irrevocably things could change.

But perhaps, she thought, her throat tightening, I'll be the one to leave instead. Find a new life with different challenges.

Or perhaps Patrick would take her in his arms and tell her, 'You're going nowhere. You're staying here with me.'

And wished she found that more of a comfort.

She was thankful, however, when Saturday arrived, with the prospect of half a day's relief from the increasingly heavy atmosphere of the school.

As she cycled to work, it occurred to her that when she'd gone to university, her ultimate plan had been to become a teacher. But that, of course, was before Fate had sent her schemes crashing round her.

But it was something she might well reconsider now circumstances had changed.

When she sat down at her desk, she was surprised to see there was no pile of correspondence with attendant Post-it instructions waiting beside the computer.

The door to Mrs Wilding's office was closed, but Tavy could hear the faint murmur of her voice, interspersed with silences, indicating that she was on the telephone.

In which case, Tavy decided, maybe I'll pop to the staff room. Ask a few pertinent questions about getting back into higher education.

She was on her way down the corridor when she heard a door open behind her and Mrs Wilding saying, 'Octavia— a word, please.' Her tone showed that the big chill was still on, and Tavy bit her lip as she turned back.

In her office, Mrs Wilding motioned Tavy to a chair. 'I won't beat about the bush,' she said. 'I have to tell you that I no longer find our arrangement satisfactory.'

'Arrangement,' Tavy repeated, bewildered.

'Your employment here as my assistant.' The other woman spoke impatiently. 'I have therefore decided to terminate it.'

Tavy stared at her across the wide expanse of polished desk. She said slowly, 'You mean—you're firing me? But why?'

'Because the nature of the job will be changing.' Mrs Wilding examined her manicured nails. 'The school will be expanding and I require someone who shares my vision and can work closely beside me—even represent me on occasion.'

Expanding? Tavy felt her jaw dropping. Only a matter of days ago, Mrs Wilding had been prophesying doom and ruin.

With an effort, she kept her voice steady. 'And I don't qualify?'

'Oh, my dear.'

Those three little words said it all, thought Tavy. Amused, patronising and incredulous.

Mrs Wilding allowed it to sink in, then continued, 'You try hard, Octavia, within your limitations, but this was never intended to be a permanency. You needed work and, because of your sad personal circumstances, I felt duty bound to respond. But now the time has come to move on.'

She paused, looking past Tavy. 'Which I imagine you too will be doing quite soon. I was speaking to Archdeacon Christie at a social function recently and he told me that Holy Trinity's days are numbered. So this seemed a convenient moment to make a change.'

'I see.' Tavy rose shakily to her feet. 'However, I suppose you'll want me to work to the end of term?'

'Actually, no. It might be best if you cleared your desk now.' Mrs Wilding picked up an envelope, lying in front of her. 'I have made out a cheque to cover your remuneration for the period in question, and enclosed a reference which you may find helpful.'

She paused again. Smiled. Pure, undiluted vinegar. 'And please believe that I wish you well in the future, Octavia, wherever your path leads.'

She added with telling significance, 'But you must always have known it could never be here.'

In that instant, Tavy knew that she was referring to Patrick. That she had probably known from the first that they were dating, might have guessed Tavy's hopes and dreams, and always intended to put a stop to it—some day, somehow. And that this was the moment she had chosen.

Tavy would have liked to tear the envelope and its contents in small pieces and throw it in Mrs Wilding's face, but the humiliating truth was that she could not afford to do so. She needed the money and whatever passed for a recommendation in her employer's opinion. She didn't flatter herself, of course, that it would glow with praise and goodwill.

But it was better than nothing. And repeating those words silently like a mantra got her out of the room before she actually threw up on Mrs Wilding's expensive carpeting.

The desk clearing took no time at all. There were no personal mementoes to be packed, apart from a paperback edition of *The Return of the Native* which she'd been rereading during her lunch-breaks.

All the same, she was shocked to find Mrs Wilding waiting in the passage when she emerged from her tiny cramped office, as if she was guilty of some misdemeanour and needed to be escorted from the premises. She took her bag from her shoulder and held it out.

'Perhaps you'd like to search it,' she suggested, lifting her chin defiantly. 'Make sure some errant paper clip hasn't strayed in.'

Mrs Wilding's lips tightened. 'There is no need for insolence, Octavia. Although your attitude makes me see how right I am to dispense with your services—such as they are.'

Tavy found herself being conducted inexorably to the rear door, and the sound of it closing behind her possessed an almost terrifying finality.

No job, she thought numbly, as she retrieved her bicycle,

mounted it and headed, not as steadily as usual, down the
drive. No man, and soon—no home. Or, at least, not the one
she knew and loved.

It was one thing to be considering a change in your circumstances, she thought, as she turned out of the gate. Quite
another to have it forced upon you at a moment's notice.

Patrick, she whispered under her breath. *Patrick.*

Did he know what his mother was planning? Was that
the reason behind this week of silence? No, she couldn't—
wouldn't—believe it. If he'd been aware of what was happening, she was sure he'd have warned her.

Or would he? She just didn't know any more.

It occurred to her too that if she suddenly showed up at
the Vicarage at this hour, her father, immersed as usual in
his sermon, would know something was wrong.

And, remembering Mrs Wilding's silky comments about
her conversation with the Archdeacon, Tavy flinched at telling him that all the news was bad.

He has enough on his plate just now, she told herself defensively. I won't even mention that I've been sacked. I'll wait
and choose a more appropriate time—for preference when I
have the prospect of other work. I'll go over to Market Tranton on Monday morning and see what the Job Centre has to
offer—waitressing, shelf-stacking, anything.

But for now, she needed a bolt-hole, and the church was
the only place she could think of where she could be seen
without arousing comment.

She parked her bicycle in the porch, and opened the door,
thankful that the building was never locked in the daytime,
and discovering to her relief that she had it to herself, offering her a brief respite in order to calm down and gather
her thoughts.

She chose a side pew in the shelter of a pillar, and sat,
staring into space, breathing in the pleasant odours of candle
wax and furniture polish, waiting for some of the icy chill

inside her to disperse. Although the glorious blast of crimson from each end of the altar did nothing to help, showing her that her unwanted roses were still in full bloom when she'd hoped they'd be long gone.

That would have been one positive step, she thought and felt the acrid taste of tears in her throat.

She leaned a shoulder against the pillar, eyes closed, struggling desperately for control, and heard someone ask, 'Are you all right?'

Only it wasn't just 'someone' but the last person in the world she wanted to see or hear.

Reluctantly, she straightened and forced herself to look up at Jago Marsh. No black today, she noticed, but a pair of pale chinos topped by a white shirt. To show off his tan presumably, she thought, her mouth drying.

'What are you doing here?' Her voice sounded strained and husky.

'I arrived earlier,' he said. 'I wanted to sketch that rather nice pulpit. And do some quiet thinking.'

'Sketching?' she repeated. 'You?' Then paused. 'Oh— you went to art school. I'd forgotten.'

He grinned. 'I'm flattered you bothered to find out.' He paused. 'But let's get back to you, my fellow refugee. Why are you here?'

'My father said some of the kneelers needed mending,' Tavy improvised swiftly. 'I came in to collect them.'

'I saw you creep in,' he said. 'You didn't look like a woman with a mission. More as if you wanted somewhere to hide.'

She said shortly, 'Now you're being ridiculous.' And rose to her feet, thankful that she hadn't allowed her feelings of pain and insecurity to cause her to break down altogether.

'Well, I must be getting on,' she added with a kind of insane brightness, unhooking the kneeler from the pew in front.

'Are you intending to repair them here?'

'No, I'll take them back to the Vicarage,' said Tavy, wishing now that she'd picked some other—any other—excuse for her presence.

'I have the car outside. I'll give you a hand.'

'That won't be necessary.'

The tawny eyes glinted. 'Planning on transporting them one at a time?' he enquired affably.

'No,' she said, tautly. 'Deciding the repairs can wait.'

'Very wise,' he said. 'You can show me round the church instead.'

'It's hardly big enough to merit a guided tour.' She gestured round her. 'What you see is what you get. Plain and simple.' She paused. 'And I'm sure there's a whole section about it in the book Dad lent you.'

'Indeed there was,' he said. 'For instance, I know it was built by Henry Manning, the owner of Ladysmere just after Queen Victoria came to the throne. He gave the land and paid for the work, also adding a peal of bells to the tower in memory of his eldest son who was killed at Balaclava.'

'Yes,' she said. 'William Manning. There's a plaque on the wall over there. But now there's only one bell, rung before services. The others were removed several years ago.'

'People objected to the noise?'

'No, nothing like that. As a matter of fact, everyone was very sad about it. But it turned out the tower just wasn't strong enough to support them any longer.'

He frowned. 'That sounds serious.'

'Yes,' she said. 'It is. Very. But it's not your problem. Now, if you'll excuse me…'

'To do what? Count the hymn books?' He paused. 'Or change the altar flowers, perhaps.' His faint smile did not reach his eyes. 'They must be past their best by now.'

Tavy's face warmed. 'The flowers aren't my responsibility,' she said, replacing the kneeler.

'Tell me, do you recycle all your unwanted bouquets in this way?'

'I don't get flowers as a rule.' She gave him a defiant look. 'As I said—I assumed it was a mistake.'

He said silkily, 'But one that won't be repeated, if that's any reassurance.'

'And now I'll go,' she went on. 'And let you return to sketching.'

'I've done enough for one morning. I'll drive you back to the Vicarage instead.'

Oh, no, she fretted silently. It was still much too early for that.

'Thanks, but I'm not going straight home.'

'Ah,' he said. 'Could I be interrupting some assignation?'

Her breath caught. 'Please don't be absurd.'

He said slowly, brows lifting, 'Anyway, you work on Saturday mornings. Is that why you're lurking in here—hiding away—because you're skiving off? Playing truant from school?' He tutted. 'What would your father say?'

She said hoarsely, 'I'm more concerned about how he'll react when he hears I've been fired. Thrown out on my ear.' Her voice cracked suddenly. 'Just as if things weren't bad enough already.'

And, all her good intentions suddenly blown, she sank down on to the pew and began to cry. Not just a flurry of tears but harsh, racking sobs that burnt her throat, and which she could not control.

And in front of *him*. Of all people.

She would never recover from the shame of it. Or from the knowledge that he was now sitting beside her. That his arm was round her, pulling her to him so that her wet face was buried against his shoulder. So that she was inhaling the warm musk of his skin through the fabric of his shirt with every uneven gasping breath, as she struggled for composure, and for a semblance of sanity, as she realised his free hand was stroking her hair, gently and rhythmically.

When the sobs eventually choked into silence, she drew away, and he released her instantly, passing her an immaculate linen handkerchief.

Sitting rigidly upright, she blotted her face, and blew her nose, trying to think of something to say.

But all that she could come up with was a mumbled, 'I'm sorry.'

'What do you have to apologise for? I'd have thought the boot was on quite a different foot.'

'I mean I'm sorry for making such a fool of myself.'

'You've had a shock.' His tone was matter-of-fact. 'Under the circumstances, I'd say tears were a normal human reaction.' He paused. 'So what were the grounds for your dismissal? Have you had the usual verbal and written warnings?'

Tavy shook her head. 'Nothing like that. She just told me I wasn't up to the job as she saw it, handed me a cheque and told me to go.' She swallowed another sob. 'But what's going to happen to the office? She has no idea about the computer. I don't think she even knows how to switch it on.'

'I wouldn't worry. I'm sure she has your successor already in place.' He watched her absorb that, and nodded. 'However she's driven a horse and cart through your statutory rights. You could take her to a tribunal.'

Tavy shuddered. 'No—I really couldn't. I simply want to find another job and get on with my life.'

He was silent for a moment, then: 'So what else has gone wrong?'

She looked around her. 'It's this,' she said in a low voice. 'Dad's church. It needs thousands of pounds in repairs, and the diocese can't afford it. We were hoping for a reprieve but it's going to be closed. So we'll be leaving.'

She swallowed. 'She—Mrs Wilding—told me so, as part

of her justification for getting rid of me. She knows the Archdeacon.'

There was a silence, then Jago said softly, 'She's a real piece of work, your ex-boss. I wouldn't want a daughter of mine to go to her school.'

A daughter of mine...

Something that was almost pain twisted deep inside her, as she tried to imagine him as a father—and, of course, a husband, which was ludicrous with his track record. He could never settle for anything so conventional, she told herself vehemently. And heaven help anyone who hoped he'd change.

'Well, there's no chance of that,' she said with sudden crispness, as she rallied herself. 'She thinks you're Satan's less nice brother.'

'Then maybe I should immediately withdraw from this sacred place to more appropriate surroundings,' he drawled. 'Come with me to the pub and have a drink. I think you could use one.'

'No,' she said, too quickly. 'Thank you, but I really should get back and talk to Dad. It won't help to delay things.'

He walked beside her as she wheeled her bike down to the gate.

'Tell me,' he said. 'What does your boyfriend think of his mother's decision?'

Tavy bit her lip. 'I—I don't think he knows.'

'How convenient.'

The note of contempt in his voice stung.

She turned on him. 'Patrick will be devastated when he hears,' she said hotly. 'And, anyway, just what business is it of yours? How dare you walk into this village, making assumptions, passing judgements on people you barely know?'

'Because outsiders can often see the whole picture,' Jago returned, unruffled. 'Whereas you, my sweet, are incapable of looking further than the end of your charming nose.'

'You know nothing,' she hurled back at him, her voice

shaking. 'Nothing at all. You've mixed in dirt for so long, you can't recognise or appreciate decency.'

'Ah,' he said softly. 'Back to that, are we? If that's the case, what do I have to lose?'

One stride brought him within touching distance, his fingers gripping her slender shoulders, rendering her immobile. He bent his head and his mouth took hers in a long hard kiss that sent strange echoes reverberating through every nerve of her body, and sent the world spinning helplessly out of synch.

His lips urged hers apart, allowing his tongue to invade her mouth's inner sweetness and explore it with a fierce and sensual insistence totally unlike his previous gentleness. It was impossible to breathe—to think. Or, even, to resist...

At the same time, his hands slid down to her hips, jerking her forward, grinding her slender body against his. Making her shockingly aware that he was passionately and shamelessly aroused.

And, worse still, making her want to press even closer to him. To wind her arms round his neck and feel the silky gloss of his hair under her fingers. To make the kiss last for ever...

When he finally released her, she was trembling inside, with fury that she had not been the one to step back first, and disbelief at her body's own reaction to this stark introduction to desire.

She wanted to call him a brute and a bastard, but somehow her voice wouldn't work.

He, of course, had no such problem. He said harshly, the tawny gaze scorching her, 'A word of advice. Open your eyes, Octavia, before it's too late.'

Then he turned and crossed the road to where a Jeep was parked under a chestnut tree, swung himself into the driver's seat, and roared off without a backward glance.

Leaving her staring after him, a shaking hand pressed to her swollen mouth.

CHAPTER EIGHT

It was a subdued afternoon. Lloyd Denison listened gravely to everything Tavy had to say, although she kept back her encounter with Jago and its shameful aftermath, then retired to his study with the comment, 'She does not deserve you, my dear, and never did.'

He was distressed for her, thought Tavy, but not particularly surprised.

She did her best to be upbeat, checking online that she had the requisite qualifications to train for a B.Ed, although she found with dismay that she'd have to wait until September to apply for the following year.

Which meant she had to find some way to support herself in the interim period.

And, to her bewilderment, there was still no word from Patrick, making it difficult to altogether dismiss Jago's unpleasant comments.

I'll just have to tackle him myself, she thought.

Accordingly, after breakfast the following morning, she asked if she might absent herself from Morning Prayer and borrow the Peugeot. 'There's something I need to do.'

'Yes, of course you may.' Mr Denison studied her for a moment. 'Want to tell me about it?'

She forced a smile. 'Not right now.'

Market Tranton's streets were quiet as Tavy made her way across town to the modern block where Patrick had his flat. She was just about to turn into the parking lot when a car pulled out in front of her, forcing her to brake sharply.

It was a convertible with the hood up, but she recognised it instantly, as it sped off. It was Fiona Culham's car, and she was driving it, wearing sunglasses and with a scarf tied over her blonde hair.

Tavy sat very still for a moment, aware that her pulses were drumming oddly, as she told herself that there was probably a perfectly logical explanation, and that driving straight back to Hazelton Magna was the coward's way out.

Then, taking a deep breath, she turned into the car park and found another car hurriedly departing, leaving an empty bay. An elderly woman was just emerging from the main entrance as she arrived, and she held the door open with a friendly smile. Tavy took the stairs to the first floor, and rang Number Eleven's bell.

Patrick answered the door almost immediately. He was bare-legged, wearing a towelling robe and an indulgent smile.

'So, what have you forgotten…?' he began, then paused gaping as he registered his visitor's identity. 'Tavy—what the hell are you doing here?'

'I think it's called "wising up".' She couldn't believe how calm she sounded when, by rights, she should be falling apart. 'May I come in?'

There was another pause, then he reluctantly stood aside. She walked into the living room and looked around. The table in the window still held the remnants of breakfast for two, while the bedroom door was open affording a clear view of the tumbled bed.

'So,' she said. 'You and Fiona.'

'Yes,' he said. 'As it happens. I didn't know you'd been spying on us.'

'Spying?' she echoed incredulously. 'Don't be ridiculous.

I had no idea until I saw her driving away.' She paused. 'When did it start?'

'Does it matter?' His tone was defensive. He looked uncomfortable. Even shifty.

'I think I'm entitled to ask.'

'Oh, for heaven's sake,' he said impatiently. 'You're a nice kid, Tavy, but it was never really serious between us. Surely you realised that.'

She said quietly, 'I'm beginning to. But what I can't quite figure is why "we" happened at all.'

He shrugged. 'When I came down here, I needed a local girlfriend, and you…filled the bill.'

'And was that why we only met outside the village—so that you could dump me for Fiona without looking quite so much of a bastard?'

'Oh, do we really have to pick it all over?' he asked irritably. 'Let's just say we had some nice times together and leave it there. Things change.'

Yes, thought Tavy. I've lost my job. I may lose my home and now I've lost you—except it seems that I never had you in the first place.

She lifted her chin. Smiled. 'In that case,' she said. 'Let me wish you both every happiness.' She paused. 'I presume you will be getting married.'

'Yes, when her divorce is finally settled, among other things.' He didn't smile back. 'Until then, perhaps you'd be good enough to keep your mouth shut about us.'

'Who,' she asked, 'could I possibly want to tell?'

And walked out, closing the door behind her.

She drove steadily back to Hazelton Magna. About a mile from the village she pulled over on to the verge, switched off the engine and sat for a while trying to gather her thoughts and gauge her own reactions. Waiting, too, for the pain to strike as if she'd just deliberately bitten down on an aching tooth.

After all, Patrick was the man she'd believed she was in love with—wasn't he?

Only, there was nothing. Not even a sense of shock. Just a voice in her head saying, 'So that's it.' Rather like being handed the solution to a puzzle—interesting, but not particularly important.

Looking back with new and sudden clarity, she could see she'd been flattered by Patrick's attentions because of the memory of that long-ago crush.

She'd let herself think a new chapter had opened in her life. Yet how in the world could she have mistaken lukewarm for passionate? Except, of course, she had no benchmark for comparison. Or, at least, not then…

No, don't go there.

Switching her mind determinedly back to Patrick, she could see now why there had been no pressure from him to consummate their relationship. Not consideration as she'd thought but indifference.

My God, she thought wryly. Even Dad saw that I was fooling myself.

And so did Jago…

Jago…

Even the whisper of his name made her tremble.

Now, there she could find pain, she thought. Pain that was immeasurably deep and frighteningly intense. Even life-changing. The certainty of it tightened her throat and set her pulses thudding crazily.

Patrick's kisses had been enjoyable but had always left her aware she should have wanted more but wondering about her uncertainty. Yet the mere brush of Jago's mouth on hers had opened a door into her senses that she'd never dreamed could exist. Offered a lure as arousing as it was dangerous.

And he hadn't even been trying. In fact, he'd probably been amusing himself by gauging the precise depth of her innocence.

Maybe because he too thought she was 'a nice kid', she told herself, and flinched.

Hang on to that thought, she adjured herself almost feverishly. That's the way to armour yourself against him, because you must do that. No out of the frying pan into the fire for you, my girl.

Tomorrow you go back to Market Tranton and you find a job stacking shelves or anything else that offers pay.

And you forget the past, disregard the present and concentrate on the future.

'Was Mrs Wilding at church?' she asked her father later as she dished up their lunch of lamb steaks with new potatoes and broccoli.

'Fortunately, no,' Mr Denison said, helping himself to mint sauce. 'I imagine she'll be transferring her allegiance to Saint Peter's in Gunslade for the duration.'

Tavy stared at him. 'But, Dad, she's on the parochial church council.'

'Yes, my dear, but that always had more to do with establishing her position in the village than anything else.' He paused. 'Did I mention that Julie Whitman and her fiancé were coming this afternoon at two-thirty to discuss their wedding? It could well be Holy Trinity's last marriage service, so we'll have to find some way to make it special.'

'Oh, don't say that.' Tavy shook her head. 'Maybe if we got up a petition…'

'I don't think so, darling. I'm afraid we have to bow to the inevitable, however unwelcome.'

Once the apple crumble which followed the lamb had been disposed of, Tavy cleared away, loaded the elderly dishwasher, and took her coffee into the garden. As she stepped on to the lawn, she heard the front doorbell sound in the distance. Julie and Graham had arrived early, she thought with a faint smile.

It was a warm day with only a light breeze and she wandered round, looking at the garden as if seeing it for the first time, kicking off her shoes to feel the fresh, sweet grass under her bare feet. Wondering if the lilac and laburnum had ever been so lovely and breathing in the scent of the early roses. Trying to capture a lifetime of memories in a moment.

She was under no illusions as to what would happen to the garden. The whole site would be bought up by a developer who would demolish the rambling inconvenient house, and use all the land to build a collection of bijou village residences. And she hoped she would be miles away when that happened, she thought fiercely.

She sat down under the magnolia on the ancient wooden bench she'd been planning to repaint and sipped her cooling coffee.

A wave of weariness swept over her. The day's revelations had taken their toll after all. Nor had she slept well the night before. Snatches of her disturbing dreams kept coming back to her, and she was glad she could not remember the rest of them.

Above her the magnolia blossoms shivered, and, through half-closed lids, she saw a shadow fall across the grass in front of her.

Her eyes snapped open and she sat up with a jerk, nearly spilling the remains of her coffee when she realised who was standing there.

She said breathlessly, 'How did you get in here?'

Jago shrugged. 'I rang the doorbell in the conventional way, was greeted by your father and chatted to him until the would-be-weds arrived when he sent me out here to find you. Is there a problem?'

She glared at him. 'It didn't occur to you that you're the last person I want to see?' *And especially when I'm wearing the old denim skirt and washed out T-shirt I'd have once opted for.*

'Yes,' he said. 'But I didn't let it trouble me for long.'

She said coldly, 'I suppose you've come to apologise.'

'Why? For suggesting you wake up and smell the coffee, or for kissing you? If so, you'll be disappointed. I have no regrets on either count.' Uninvited, he sat down on the grass, stretching long legs in front of him.

More chinos today, she noticed unwillingly, and a shirt the colour of a summer sky.

'Has the man at the top of your welcome list put in an appearance?'

'No,' said Tavy, fighting an urge to grind her teeth. 'Nor is he likely to.'

'Ah,' he said, and gave her a thoughtful glance. 'So you know.'

'Yes,' she admitted curtly.

'How did you find out?'

'I went over to his flat this morning—to talk.' She lifted her chin. 'She was—just leaving. It was clear she'd been there all night.'

He said quietly, 'And you're upset.'

'I'm devastated,' she said defiantly. 'Naturally.'

Jago's dark brows lifted. 'Then I can only say—I'm sorry.'

There was a silence, then Tavy said, 'Tell me something. How did you find out?'

'I became suspicious that night in the pub. She was so insistent we go there, and then the landlord told me they'd been quarrelling at the bar, and she'd been winding him up, apparently about being with me.

'I also have the hidden advantage of knowing Fiona's soon-to-be ex-husband,' he added calmly. 'We've had dinner a couple of times in London. I learned a lot about his brief marriage including his conviction that she'd been seeing someone else almost from the start. A boyfriend from the old days.'

Tavy moved uncomfortably. 'But as they're getting divorced, anyway...'

'It's not that simple.' Jago shook his head. 'Apparently the Latimer family had their lawyers draw up a form of pre-nuptial agreement. Under it, Fiona gets a more than generous divorce settlement if the marriage breaks down, unless infidelity can be proved, when she only gets a fraction more than zilch.'

He shrugged. 'I believe that's why she got Patrick to leave London, in case they were being watched.'

Tavy said numbly, 'And why he needed a local girl-friend—as a smokescreen.'

'Try and look on that as a blessing,' Jago said smoothly. 'It could have been worse.'

She bit her lip. 'Is that why you're here? To tell me all this?'

'Not at all.'

'Then what do you want?' she demanded.

'I came to offer you a job.'

There was a silence, then Tavy said unevenly, 'If this is some kind of unpleasant joke, I don't find it funny.'

'On the contrary, it's a *bona fide* offer of employment with proper hours and real wages. Work starts on the house next week, and I cannot always be around to oversee it, so I need a project manager onsite to sort out any problems as soon as they happen and make sure it all goes smoothly and on time.' He paused. 'Obviously, I thought of you.'

'I see nothing obvious about it. You must be mad.'

'I'm being practical,' he returned. 'You live locally, so there's no travelling involved. You're currently unemployed. You're totally trustworthy, computer literate, and you've worked capably in administration, according to your former boss's grudging reference.'

'How did you know that?' she demanded furiously.

'Your father told me. And, like me, he thinks you could

do the job easily. For one thing, the firms I've hired are all local, and you'll probably know them. That's a big plus.'

He added softly, 'I'm naturally aware that you're just waiting to tell me that you'd rather be boiled in oil than accept any help from a totally unreconstructed lowlife like me, but, in fact, I'm the one who needs your help. And all I'm asking is that you think about it.'

'I have thought,' she said. 'And the answer's "no".'

'May I ask why?'

She bit her lip. 'Because while you may have persuaded my father to trust you, I don't. So, I prefer to keep my distance.'

'And so you can,' Jago said evenly. 'Didn't you hear me say that I have to be away a great deal over the coming weeks? Which is exactly why I need a project manager at the house.'

He paused. 'Besides, you'll be company for Barbie.'

She said tautly, 'Who exactly is Barbie?'

'She's going to keep house for me.' He smiled reflectively. 'I hadn't banked on her wanting to move in so soon, but it seems she can't wait for it all to be finished.'

'How sweet,' Tavy said icily, aware that her heart had given a strange lurch. 'In which case, why not let her be project manager? She sounds ideal.'

'Oh, she is,' he said gently. 'In so many ways. Except she doesn't know one end of a computer from another. Nor does she have your all-important rapport with the locals.'

He got lithely to his feet, and smiled down at her.

'But with her around, you'd certainly be safe from any unwanted molestation, wouldn't you. If that's what you're afraid of.'

'I'm not even remotely scared,' she fired back.

'Excellent,' he said smoothly. 'That's one weight off my mind.' He paused. 'Now, I hope you'll give some reasonable thought to my proposition, and not allow yourself to be ruled by your very natural prejudice against me. You can contact me at Barkland Grange when you've made your final decision.

'As I've said—it's a job, nothing more and purely temporary.' He added softly, 'Besides, half the time you won't even know I'm there.'

Tavy watched him wander across the lawn and round the side of the house. A minute later, she heard the sound of the departing Jeep.

She leaned limply against the back of the bench, trying to calm her flurried breathing.

If it was anyone else in the world, she thought passionately, she'd seize the opportunity and be grateful. But not Jago Marsh. Not in a million years.

Manipulative swine—talking to her father first, and getting him on side before approaching her.

And how could she now explain to Dad that the situation was impossible without involving the additional explanations she was so anxious to avoid?

Sighing, she glanced at her watch, realising the wedding chat would be drawing to its close and it was probably time she took a tray of tea and biscuits to the study.

And by the time Julie and Graham left, she would probably have amassed a list of perfectly acceptable reasons, excluding all personal stuff, why working at Ladysmere would be a bad idea. Or enough to convince her father that she was making a considered, rational decision.

And now all I have to do to convince myself, she thought as she returned to the house.

As it turned out, she'd forgotten that this was the Sunday that her father went to take Communion to the local Care Home, so she had no chance to speak to him until after Evensong, over their supper of cheese salad.

She said abruptly, 'Dad, I can't accept this job offer at Ladysmere.'

Her father helped himself to mayonnaise. 'I'm sorry to hear that, darling. Any particular reason?'

All the carefully formulated excuses vanished like morning mist. Astonished, she heard herself say, 'Jago Marsh made a pass at me.'

'This afternoon?'

'Well—no. The other day.' She ate a piece of tomato. 'You don't seem too surprised.'

'Why should I be?' His smile was gentle. 'You're a very lovely girl, Octavia.'

She flushed. 'Then surely you must see why I want to avoid him.'

He said quietly, 'I think, my dear, that if you plan to steer clear of every man who finds you attractive, you're doomed to spend the next years of your life in permanent hiding.'

She stared at him. 'Hardly, Dad. You seem to forget I've been—seeing someone.'

'Believe me, I've forgotten nothing,' her father said with a touch of grimness. 'But we've seen so little of Patrick Wilding lately that I'd begun to wonder.'

Tavy bent her head. 'Well, you don't have to. I won't be seeing him any more.'

'I see,' her father said and sighed. 'It's a great pity I let you leave university. I love this village but I've always known it was something of an ivory tower, and you needed to expand your horizons. You'd have soon developed a strategy for dealing with any unwanted admirers.' He paused. 'And, more importantly, to differentiate between them and the real thing.'

She bit her lip. 'Well, Jago Marsh will always be the wrong thing.' She hesitated. 'Did he tell you that he has some woman moving into the Manor?'

'He mentioned it.' Mr Denison pushed away his empty plate and reached for the *cafetière*. 'I'd have thought that would dispel your anxieties.'

She swallowed. 'Then—in spite of everything—you really think I should take this job?'

He shrugged. 'At least it would be a well-paid stopgap for you until we find out what the future holds.'

He paused, reflectively. 'And he's certainly a multitalented young man. Did you know that he's been doing some sketches of Holy Trinity's interior?'

'He mentioned it, yes.'

'He showed them to me. And he gave me this, too.' He reached into the folder holding his sermon notes and extracted a sheet torn from a drawing block.

Tavy, expecting to see the extravagantly carved pulpit or the font, felt her jaw drop. Because the sketch was of a girl, sitting in the shadow of a pillar, her expression wistful, almost lost.

It's me, she thought. Me to the life.

She said shakily, 'He is good. It's like looking in a mirror.'

Her father said gently, 'But I could wish there was a happier face looking back at you.'

She bit her lip. 'There will be, I promise.'

When she'd cleared the supper things, Tavy telephoned Barkland Grange, and asked to be connected to Jago Marsh's suite.

'Your name, please?'

'Octavia Denison,' she returned reluctantly.

'Oh, yes, Miss Denison, Mr Marsh is expecting your call.'

Tavy, horrified, was strongly tempted to slam the phone down, but Jago was already answering.

'It's good to hear from you,' he said. 'Is it a hopeful sign?'

She said stiffly, 'I've decided to take the job after all if that's what you mean.'

'Excellent,' he said calmly. 'I'd be glad if you could be at the house tomorrow morning at eight-thirty.'

She gasped. 'So soon?'

'Of course. Ted Jackson will already be there, and he'll

give you a key for your own use. I've been using the former
library as an office, and the computer has a broadband con-
nection. You'll find a preliminary list of the items that need
your attention and the names of the firms I've hired so far.

'The heating engineers will be arriving tomorrow to
install a new boiler, and I'm expecting someone from the
plumbing company to prepare an estimate for turning part
of the master suite into a bathroom. Can you handle that?'

'Yes,' she managed. 'I think so.'

'The kitchen's perfectly usable at the moment,' he went
on. 'No doubt regular supplies of tea and coffee will be
needed when work starts, so you'd better stock up, making
a note of everything you spend.'

He paused again. 'Now I'll say goodnight, but please believe, Octavia, that I'm sincerely grateful to you.'

There was a click and he was gone, leaving Tavy feeling
limp, as if she'd had a close encounter with a tornado. Brisk
and businesslike to the nth degree with not even a hint of
the personal touch, she thought, gasping. But surely that was
what she wanted? Wasn't it?

Wasn't it...?

And couldn't find an answer that made any kind of sense.

CHAPTER NINE

IT SEEMED STRANGE to be walking up the Manor's drive to the main entrance rather than sneaking in through the no-longer-broken side gate. Strange, but infinitely safer.

Glancing around, Tavy saw that Ted Jackson and his gang had already done wonders in the grounds. Bushes and shrubs had been ruthlessly cut back to reveal what would once again be herbaceous borders, and a drastic weeding programme was in progress. The lawns had clearly been scythed and were now being mown and rolled.

She imagined work would also have started on the lake, but she was damned if she was going down there to find out. Forbidden territory, she told herself sternly, managing a smile as Ted Jackson appeared.

'Well, you're an early bird and no mistake,' he said genially. 'My missus couldn't get over it when Mr Marsh rang last night, and said you'd be working here.'

And will now be busily spreading the news on the bush telegraph, Tavy thought, gritting her teeth.

'Funny old business up at the school,' he went on with relish. 'My June says she can't imagine Mrs Wilding and that Culham girl seeing eye to eye for very long. Fireworks pretty soon, she reckons.'

Tavy felt her jaw drop. Fiona, she thought with disbelief. *Fiona*—hardly one of the world's workers—had taken her place and become the new PA?

Aware that her reaction to the news was being watched with keen interest, she pulled herself together. Even shrugged. 'Not my problem, I'm thankful to say. But I mustn't keep you.'

'And when Mr Marsh gets in touch, tell him Bob Wyatt can start on the conservatory tomorrow,' he added, handing her a key.

Tavy frowned. 'What's going to happen to it?'

'He's going to use it as a studio for his painting, seemingly. The right light, or some such.'

Another piece of information she hadn't been expecting, Tavy thought, turning away. Yet becoming a professional artist was, presumably, the new beginning he'd once mentioned.

As she let herself into the house, her first impression was that the cleaners had done an impressive job, although their efforts couldn't hide peeling wallpaper and shabby paintwork. And in spite of the fresh scent of cleaning liquid and polish, the overall impression was still one of neglect, she thought, carrying her bulging carrier bags down the long corridor to the kitchen at the back of the house.

She put the teabags, coffee and paper cups in the massive dresser, and placed the milk into the elderly, cumbersome fridge.

She made herself a coffee and carried it to the library, now just a room with a lot of empty shelves, and hoped with a pang that Sir George's books had found good homes.

There was a large table in the middle of the room holding a smart new laptop, plus a printer and a telephone, while, under the window, was a stationery trolley with printer paper, notebooks, pens and markers, and two large box files, one containing quotations, the other catalogues mainly for white goods, furniture and bathroom equipment.

When she switched on the laptop, there was mail waiting. Hesitantly, she clicked on the icon and read, 'I hope you had a restful night with sweet dreams.'

She swallowed, knowing how far that was from the truth. Because some of last night's dreams, which she was still embarrassed to remember, had been far from conventionally sweet. In fact they'd provided the incentive for today's early start.

Because she'd been driven into getting up, afraid to go back to sleep in case she once again experienced a man's warm, hard body pressing her into the softness of the mattress, or found herself drinking from his kisses and breathing the heated, unmistakable fragrance of his skin as she lifted herself towards him in silent yearning for his possession.

Fantasies, she thought, that were the total opposite of restful and should never be recalled in daylight. But at least she'd never seen his face or put a name to her dream lover.

She took a deep breath and went on reading.

I suggest you spend some time today going over the place so that you're thoroughly familiar with the layout. Open any mail that comes, deal with what you can, put the rest aside for my attention.

In case any serious problems arise and you need backup, I'm sending you my contact details, but these are strictly for your personal use, not to be disclosed to anyone else.

I'm using the master bedroom as temporary storage for my painting stuff until work on the studio is finished.

I have as yet no firm idea when Barbie will be arriving, but you'll find new linen in the adjoining room, which I'd like you to prepare for her, together with the bathroom opposite, and make sure there are always fresh flowers waiting.

He signed it simply 'Jago' adding his email address and mobile number underneath, together with the PS, 'I shall be dropping in occasionally to check progress.'

And no doubt to check on Barbie too, thought Tavy, her mouth tightening, wondering why he didn't drop the pretence and simply move the lady into the master bedroom from day or perhaps night one.

It occurred to her that perhaps Barbie was the girl that he'd fought over with Pete Hilton. If so, it must be a serious relationship to have lasted this long, and not one of many casual sexual encounters as he'd implied.

On the other hand, she was here to do a job, not to brood on her employer's morals, such as they were. And as she was scheduled to leave at six each evening, she would not, with luck, be around to witness their reunion.

Long before the end of the day, Tavy felt as if she'd been taking part in a marathon and was due to finish last.

Because the task ahead of her was larger and more complex than she'd imagined, she realised as she downloaded and printed off Jago's instructions for the work he was commissioning.

In spite of herself, she was impressed. He didn't appear to have missed a thing. And, for the first time, she began to believe that buying Ladysmere was not simply a momentary whim. That this care and attention to detail indicated that he really intended to make it his home. A place where he would settle down and perhaps raise a family.

An odd shiver went down her spine at the prospect and, for a moment, she sat staring into space with eyes that saw nothing.

But she swiftly reminded herself that, whatever his plans, they were no concern of hers. By the time they came to fruition, she would be far away and recent events would seem like a bad dream.

Then, as if a starting pistol had been fired, the phone began to ring, one call following another, while the doorbell signalled the arrival of the heating engineers. After that, there was a constant stream of people bringing books of wallpaper and fabric patterns as well as large books of carpet samples.

Giving 'home shopping' a whole new slant, thought Tavy ironically, as the empty shelves in the library began to fill up.

The plumber arrived just as she was finishing her lunch of cheese and tomato sandwiches, and she conducted him upstairs and along the passage to the imposing pair of double doors leading to the master suite, thankful to escape from the banging from the boiler room in the cellar.

It was dim inside the room, most of the light being blocked by heavy tasselled blinds. Tavy went to the windows and raised them, while the plumber disappeared through a communicating door into the soon-to-be converted dressing room to begin his calculations.

It was a big room, its size diminished by the dark, formal wallpaper which in turn detracted from the elaborate and beautiful plaster frieze above it. On the wall facing the door was a massive four-poster bed, standing like a skeleton, stripped of its canopy, mattress and curtains, but still dominating its surroundings.

Tavy walked over to take a closer look. It was a beautiful thing, she thought, running her hand down a smooth post, which like the panelled headboard set into the wall, was constructed from mellow golden oak.

Clearly an attempt had been made to pry the bed loose because it was slightly damaged.

Jago Marsh's orders, no doubt, she told herself. Not quite his image, a bed like this, and certainly no love nest for someone named after a plastic doll. No, he'd want something emperor-sized with black satin sheets...

And stopped there, wrenching herself back to reality.

What the hell do you know about men and what they want? she asked herself with derision.

When you've only been kissed with real passion once

in your life—and that was by the wrong man because he was angry.

Aware her heartbeat had quickened, she went back to the window and unfastened it, pushing it open to dispel the faint mustiness in the air.

As she turned, she noticed an easel, together with a stack of portfolios and even canvases leaning against a wall, and remembered what Jago had said about storage.

She was sorely tempted to have a look at them and see if his painting was as good as his drawing, but restrained herself with an effort. Like so much else in his life, it was none of her business.

Calling to the plumber that she'd be next door, she went reluctantly into the room designated as Barbie's, which seemed the only furnished room in the house. There was a round table holding a pink-shaded lamp, a neat chest of drawers, a small armchair upholstered and cushioned in moss green, a sheepskin rug, and of course the bed—brand-new and double-sized, its mattress still in its protective wrapping. As was the bedding, the sheets pale pink and the quilt and pillow cases white, sprigged with pink rosebuds, with matching curtains already hanging at the window.

'Very romantic,' she muttered, as she tore off the wrappings, nearly breaking a nail in the process.

She made up the bed with the precision of a mathematical formula, checked the fitted wardrobe in one corner for hangers, then put soap and towels in the old-fashioned bathroom across the passage.

'Lot of space in that dressing room,' observed the plumber as he emerged from the master suite. 'How about a bath as well as a shower because there's plenty of space? And what about fittings—chrome or gold?' He paused. 'And I've brought some tile samples on the van. Italian—top of the range.'

'They sound lovely,' said Tavy. 'And I'll ask Mr Marsh to contact you about the rest.'

'It's usually the lady that decides that kind of thing.' He grinned at her. 'Doesn't he trust you?'

Colour rose in her face. 'I shan't be living here. I'm simply the project manager.'

His glance was frankly sceptical as he turned away. 'Just as you say, love.'

The tile samples went to fill another gap on the shelves and Tavy was just adding the queries about bathroom fixtures and fittings to the email she planned to send Jago, when the doorbell rang, only to sound another prolonged and more imperious summons as she reached the hall.

Patience is a virtue, she recited under her breath as she threw open the front door, only to come face to face with Fiona Culham.

'And about time,' Fiona began, then halted, staring. 'Octavia? What the hell are you doing here?'

'Working,' said Tavy. 'I lost my job so Jago offered me another.'

The other girl's eyes narrowed. 'Presumably your father has somehow convinced him that charity begins at home.' She took a step forward. 'Now, if you'll be good enough to stand aside, I'd like a word with him.'

'I'm afraid Jago—Mr Marsh—isn't here, Miss Culham. He's away on business.'

'But he must have left a contact number.' Fiona walked past her into the hall. 'You can give me that.'

'I'm sorry,' Tavy said politely. 'But I've been instructed it's for my use only.'

Fiona gave the slightly metallic laugh that Tavy hated. 'Aren't you getting a little above yourself? This must be your first day in the job.'

'Yours too, I believe.'

There was a simmering silence, then Fiona said, 'I suppose I can leave a message.'

'Certainly. I'll get my notebook.'

'I'd prefer a sheet of paper.' Fiona took a pen from her handbag. 'And an envelope, please.'

Tavy nodded. 'I'll get them for you.'

As she reached the office, the telephone was ringing, the caller being the electrician with a preliminary quotation which he would confirm in writing.

Tavy made a note of the details, collected the stationery and returned to the hall, only to find it empty. For a moment she thought that Fiona had got tired of waiting and left, then the sound of footsteps alerted her and she saw the other girl coming down the stairs.

'I needed the bathroom,' she announced. 'Hope you don't mind.'

'I would have shown you...'

'Unnecessary.' Fiona's smile held an odd satisfaction. 'I've been a visitor here so many times, I know the place like the back of my hand.'

She wrote swiftly on the paper, folded it and put it in the envelope, sealing it with meticulous care before handing it over. 'I must emphasise this is strictly confidential.'

Tavy nodded. 'There's a lot of it about,' she said, and received a venomous look in return.

'Then, on that understanding, let me strongly advise you to keep your mouth shut—because, if you don't, you'll find that coming here has been a terrible mistake.' Fiona paused. 'Just a friendly warning.'

The door safely closed behind the unwelcome visitor, Tavy leaned back against the heavy timbers for a moment, taking a calming breath. If that's friendly, she thought, I wouldn't like to be on the receiving end of hostile.

The Jacksons were wrong, she told herself grimly. Fiona and Mrs Wilding are a match made in heaven.

But—I will not let her get to me.

And on that heartening note, she went back to the office and began devising a spreadsheet to keep track of the renovations on a daily and weekly basis.

She broke off for a brief chat with the heating engineers before they left, the new boiler installed, then locked the door behind them and returned to the computer, glad that the house was now quiet and concentration not such a problem.

For the next hour or so she sat totally engrossed, the evening sun pouring through the window.

With a brief sigh of satisfaction, she aimed the mouse at 'Print' then paused, aware of a noise that was not just the creaks and groans of an old house settling around her but, instead, sounded uncannily like footsteps approaching.

Tavy froze, staring at the door. But I locked up, she thought, swallowing. I know I did.

But you forgot to shut the window in the master bedroom, a small voice in her head reminded her. And a clever thief would have no problem at all—apart from finding something to steal.

Picking up the phone, she went to the door. She called loudly, 'Whoever you are, I'm not alone. We'll count to three, then call the police.'

'Instead of the police, try an ambulance,' an acerbic voice returned. 'Because you've just shocked the hell out of me.' And Jago came down the passage towards her, a shadowy figure in a grey linen suit and collarless white shirt.

Tavy sagged against the door frame. 'You,' she said gasping. 'What are you doing here?'

'I was about to ask you the same thing.'

'I had some work I wanted to finish.'

'How industrious,' he said. 'I presume it's on overtime rates.'

'Not at all,' she said indignantly. 'I just wanted some peace and quiet.'

'Which I have now ruined.'

'No. The work's done and ready to print.' She hesitated. 'If you were hoping to see Barbie, she's not here yet.'

'Always a law unto herself,' he said and smiled. 'What else has been happening?'

'I have a list.' She handed it to him. 'And Ted Jackson says work on your studio will begin tomorrow.'

'Well, that's good news. At the moment I'm renting, which isn't ideal, but I can't be too choosy as I'm preparing for an exhibition in the autumn.'

Her eyes widened. 'Then you're really embarking on a new career?'

'No,' he said. 'Just returning to the life I had planned before Descent intervened. You're surprised?'

She said quickly, 'It's really none of my concern.' She pointed to the shelves. 'All these sample books arrived for you.'

'I haven't time to look at them properly now. I'll take them with me, and let you know my choices.'

She nodded and produced the envelope. 'Also Miss Culham—Fiona—brought you this.'

She watched him open it and glance over the single sheet of paper it contained. She saw his mouth tighten, then he refolded the paper and tucked it back into the envelope.

He said, 'So, she was here in person.' He paused, studying Tavy's swift flush. 'Did she upset you?'

'She was hardly sweetness and light.' She bit her lip. 'She's got my old job at the school.'

'That figures,' Jago returned laconically. He gave her another, more searching glance. 'Is it a problem?'

She looked away defensively. 'Not really. After all I always knew I wasn't the daughter-in-law of choice.'

'But if that's what you still want—hang in there. It could happen.'

She frowned. 'What are you talking about?'

'Patrick,' he said. 'And you. Plus, of course, the lovely Fiona. Because it won't last between them. In fact, if you want, I can guarantee it.'

'How?'

He shrugged casually. 'By making a play for her myself.'

'*No!*' She had no idea where the word came from, or the passion that drove it but it rocked her back on her heels. While the quizzical lift of Jago's eyebrows increased the warmth of her face to burning.

'Really?' he drawled. 'So, what's the objection?'

There was an odd note in his voice which gave Tavy the sudden feeling she was teetering on the edge of a precipice she had not known existed.

She said, stammering a little, 'Because it would be cruel—unless you were serious about her.' She paused. 'Are you?'

'Not in the slightest,' he said. 'Any more than she's serious about Patrick.'

'That's absurd. She came back here to be with him.'

Jago shook his head. 'She came back because she couldn't afford her London lifestyle, and was being pressured by her parents. In order to keep her around, her father has even become a silent partner in that school, supplying her with a career and a future husband in one move.

'He even wants to buy a piece of my land as a playing field, to save the little darlings a walk to the village. I refused his first offer. This is the second,' he added, putting the letter in his pocket. 'I'm seriously tempted to see how high he's prepared to go.

'Although he's wasting his time and money, with me and Fiona, who has no intention of staying around once the divorce is finalised.'

'How can you possibly know that?'

'Something she let slip on our way to the Willow Tree that night, along with a none too subtle hint that she was available.'

His smile was charming but edged. 'And the offer's still there, so, if you want Patrick, all you have to do is be patient. Give him a shoulder to cry on and wait for him to see the light.'

Tavy drew a shaky breath. 'That's disgusting.'

'And I thought I was being practical.'

'But what about your…Barbie,' she demanded, stumbling over the name. 'Will she understand the…practicalities, when she finds out?'

'If she finds out,' he said calmly, 'she'll undoubtedly be furious with me. But it wouldn't be the first time.'

'I can imagine.' She shook her head. 'People like you. How do you live with yourselves?'

'Money,' he said, 'is a great palliative.' He paused. 'And while we're being practical, did you warn your father you'd be working late and he'd have to self-cater?'

She shook her head. 'He's playing chess tonight with a friend in the village. Supper is included.'

'In which case, you're having dinner with me.'

She gasped. 'I'm doing nothing of the kind. I'd rather…' She stopped abruptly.

'You'd rather starve,' Jago supplied silkily. 'But I'm sure that would contravene some Factories Act or Child Labour ruling.'

She said sharply, 'I'm not a child.'

'Then stop behaving like one. We have matters concerning the house to discuss, so treat it as a business dinner. I've brought food with me.'

She stared at him. 'You have? Why?'

He said slowly, 'Because I suddenly decided I'd like to dine in my own home. Idiotic but true.' There was a silence, then he added more briskly, 'There's a rug in the Jeep, so we'll have a picnic. I suggest the dining room floor.'

She said jerkily, 'No—I won't. I couldn't.'

'Because you think I won't keep my hands to myself?' Jago sounded amused. 'Darling, you're my employee so anything untoward and you can sue me for sexual harassment. You'll never need to work again.

'Also,' he went on, 'there's a lot of serious panelling in the dining room. It's hardly the right setting for an orgy. And as you so rightly pointed out, there is Barbie to consider.

'Anyway,' he added piously. 'Aren't you expected to welcome repentant sinners back to the fold? I'm sure your father would think so.'

She bit her lip again, aware of a perilous bubble of laughter suddenly rising inside her. Even though there was nothing to laugh at. 'But only if the repentance is genuine.' She paused. 'Besides, you obviously thought you'd have the place to yourself and I'm butting in.'

He said gently, 'If you were, I wouldn't have suggested you stay. Now I'll go and get the food while you finish your printing.'

It seemed the choice had been taken out of her hands, thought Tavy, her disapproval—not only of his total lack of morality but also his high-handed arrogance—tempered by the realisation that her sandwich had been a long time ago and she was, in fact, extremely hungry.

She was closing down the computer when Jago called to her.

She sat for a moment, staring into space, then whispered, as she stood up, 'I should not be doing this.'

She arrived at the dining room door and stopped, her brows lifting in sheer incredulity. 'Candles?'

There were four of them, burning with steady golden flames in the tall silver candlesticks placed at a safe distance round the corners of the rug.

'My predecessor sold the chandelier along with everything else, so the room needed some kind of light.' Jago was kneeling, unpacking a hamper. 'I bought these last week and thought—why not do it in style?'

She said shakily, 'Why not indeed—except it's not dark yet.'

He sighed. 'Stop nitpicking, woman, and lend a hand.'

There wasn't just food in the hamper. There were plates, dishes, cutlery, even wine glasses, all in pairs, strongly suggesting that he might have hoped Barbie would indeed be there.

Instead, she thought, he was settling for second best—if she even rated that highly.

Don't think like that, she adjured herself fiercely. You're not taking part in some competition, but just filling in time before the rest of your life, so remember it.

She watched Jago arranging the food on the rug. There was smoked trout pâté, chicken pie, green salad with a small container of French dressing, plus a crusty baguette, butter and a bottle of Chablis. While, to round off the meal, there was a jar of peaches in brandy.

He looked across at her, his smile faintly crooked. 'Will this do?'

'It looks wonderful,' she said. 'Like a celebration.'

'That's just how I wanted it to be.' He drew the cork from the wine and poured it, handing her a glass. 'To Ladysmere,' he said. 'A phoenix rising from the ashes.'

'Yes,' she said. *And all because of you.* She thought it, but did not say it. 'It—it's a special moment.'

He said softly, 'Yes it is, and thank you for sharing it with me.'

The tawny gaze met hers, held it for an endless moment.

And Tavy felt her heart give a sudden, wild, and totally dangerous leap, as she raised her glass and echoed huskily, 'To Ladysmere.'

CHAPTER TEN

THE WINE WAS cool and fragrant in her mouth, and she was glad of it. Grateful too for the niceties of cutting bread and butter and pâté, which gave her a chance to steady her breathing, and generally get a grip on herself.

As they ate, she said, deliberately choosing a neutral topic, 'Sir George's cousin. Why did he strip everything out of the place if he wanted to sell it?'

Jago shrugged. 'From his incoherent ramblings when we met in Spain, I gather he'd given up all hope of a sale and opted for making a fast buck out of the remaining contents instead.

'He even tried to dismantle and flog the four-poster from the master bedroom, but fortunately that couldn't be shifted.'

'Oh,' Tavy said. 'So that's how it got damaged.'

'Yes, but I'm assured it can be repaired and I'm having a new mattress specially made.' His face hardened. 'He also confided that he hoped vandals would set fire to the house so he could claim on the insurance.'

Tavy gasped. She said hotly, 'I'm only glad Sir George never knew how vile he was.'

'You liked him, didn't you?'

Outside the window, the sunset light was fading. In the massive room, the picnic rug had become a small bright island in a sea of shadows. And in the flickering light of the candles, Jago's dark face was all planes and angles as he watched her.

It was as if they were in total isolation, cut off from the rest of the world. Not close enough to touch, yet lapped in a strange and potent intimacy.

Something was flowering deep inside her—a wish—a longing that they could stay like this for ever, his gaze locked with hers. Except that was no longer enough, because her body was stirring at the memory of his hands touching her, and her lips parting beneath his.

Pushing such thoughts away, she rushed into words. 'Sir George? Everyone liked him. He was a dear man and so good to the village.'

'A lot to live up to,' Jago said lightly as he cut into the pie.

Tavy said quickly, 'Oh, but nobody expects…' and stopped, her face warming.

'Nobody expects much from a degenerate ex-rock musician,' Jago supplied drily, placing a generous wedge of pie on a plate and handing it to her. 'Well, I can hardly blame them.'

She bent her head. 'I didn't mean that. It's just that the locals were sad, I think, that Sir George didn't have a son to come after him and hoped that Ladysmere would be sold to a family so there might be—I don't know—a new dynasty, perhaps.' She forced a smile. 'Unrealistic, I know.'

'Very. For one thing, if there were children around, the lake would need to be fenced off.' He added softly, 'And that would be a pity, don't you think?'

The lake…

She was thankful he could not see how her colour had deepened. I'll never live that down, she thought helplessly. Never.

Then took a deep breath and rallied. 'But only for a while—until they learned to swim.'

'A good point,' he agreed solemnly, leaning across to refill her glass.

She said quickly, 'I shouldn't have any more.'

'Why not? I'm the one who'll be driving later.' He grinned reminiscently. 'And as my old nanny used to say "I can't, cat won't, you must".'

'You had a nanny?' She tried to imagine it and failed.

He nodded. 'I did indeed. She was a terror too. My sister and I went in fear of our lives.'

The sister was news too. The computer biography had omitted that kind of detail.

She said haltingly, 'Do you see much of your family?'

'You mean—are they still speaking to me?' He sounded amused. 'Well, yes, but currently from a distance. Becky's married to a sheep farmer in Australia and my parents have gone out to stay with her to await the arrival of their first grandchild.'

He paused. 'Now will you tell me something?'

He was going to ask about Patrick, she thought with dismay. Ask about her emotional state and she had no idea what to say.

She said stiffly, 'If I can.'

'Do you remember how this room was furnished?'

It was the last thing she'd expected and she nearly choked on the mouthful of wine she'd taken for Dutch courage.

Recovering, she said slowly, 'Well, a huge table, of course, with extra leaves so that it could seat twenty or thirty if necessary. And a very long sideboard on the wall behind you. I think it was all Victorian mahogany.'

Jago nodded thoughtfully. 'It sounds fairly daunting. And the drawing room?'

'Oh, that had enormous Chesterfields and high-backed armchairs in brown leather, very dark and slippery.' She smiled ruefully. 'I remember sitting on them as a child and being afraid I'd slide off.' She paused. 'Why do you ask?'

He said quietly, 'Because I came here originally looking

for a bolt-hole. But I now have other reasons to live here. And my ideas about décor are changing too.'

She remembered some of the catalogues. 'No Swedish minimalism?'

'Absolutely not,' he said. 'But no nineteenth century gloom either.' He paused. 'Talking of gloom, it's starting to feel chilly.' He slipped off his jacket and passed it to her. 'Put this on.' Adding, as her lips parted in protest, 'I can't risk my project manager catching cold.'

She nodded jerkily, draping his jacket round her shoulders, letting the meal continue in silence. When she'd finished, she put her fork down with a sigh. 'That was totally delicious.'

'Now try these.' Deftly, he ladled some brandied peaches into a dish.

'You're not having any?'

He shrugged. 'I suspect the alcohol content. And, as I said, I have to drive.'

'To Barkland Grange?'

'No, I'm spending tonight in London. After that—elsewhere.'

Returning, she thought, to a life she could only guess at, and which, for so many reasons, it hurt her to contemplate. The sweet richness of the peaches suddenly tasted sour.

She got to her feet saying briskly, 'Then you'll want to get on the road.'

'Later,' he said. 'After I've taken you home.'

'Oh, no.' She heard the alarm in her voice, saw his brows lift, and temporised. 'I mean—the walk will do me good. And I have things to do here before I leave.'

'Such as?'

She said feebly, 'I left a window open upstairs.'

'Then go and close it while I pack up.' He saw her hesitate and added quite gently, 'Boss's orders, Octavia.'

In the master bedroom, she went to the window and stood for a moment, trying to control the renewed tumult of her pulses.

Because something had changed between them down in that candlelit room. Something she could neither explain nor dismiss, but which terrified her. Because for a moment she had found herself wanting to say the unbelievable—the unutterable 'Don't leave me.' Or, even worse, 'Take me with you.'

When perhaps what she really meant was 'Take me…'

What's happening to me? she wondered, drawing a quivering breath. I must be going crazy.

She closed the window, securing the catch and stood for a moment staring at her reflection, his grey jacket rendering her ghostlike in the glass. She moved her shoulders under the fabric slowly, almost yearningly, as if trying to catch some trace of him, a fragment of memory to treasure, before reaching down for a sleeve and lifting it to her face.

For ten heartbeats, she held it to her cheek, before brushing it softly across her lips.

Then she slipped off the jacket, and draping it decorously over her arm, she went downstairs, where Jago would be waiting to drive her back to the Vicarage and safety.

It was a silent journey and Tavy was thankful for it. Because she knew she did not trust herself to speak.

I'm tired, she insisted silently. That's why I feel so confused and stupid. Tomorrow I'll be back on track. Become myself again instead of this creature I do not—dare not—recognise.

Jago drove up to the Vicarage's front door and looked up at the dark house.

'Your father doesn't seem to be back yet. Shall I come in with you? Make sure everything's all right?'

'There's really no need,' she said quickly, fumbling for the handle on the passenger door. 'What could possibly happen in Hazelton Magna?'

'You tell me,' he drawled. 'It was you about to call the emergency services earlier.'

She said defensively, 'Ladysmere's a big house. Some-one might think there was stuff worth stealing.' She paused, adding stiltedly, 'Goodnight—and thank you very much for the meal.'

Pure schoolgirl, she thought, vexed and was not surprised to hear faint amusement in his voice as he replied, 'It was my pleasure.'

And my pain, she thought, her nails digging into the palms of her clenched hands as she stood alone in the dark-ened house, listening to the Jeep driving away. But didn't people say pleasure and pain were two sides of the same coin?

And realised suddenly how much she would have given never to know that.

The first thing she saw when she arrived at the house next morning was the erstwhile picnic rug draped over the back of her chair. Biting her lip, she folded it carefully and put it at the back of a shelf, out of her line of vision. Start, she thought, as you mean to go on.

She went to the kitchen, filled the kettle and put it to boil, then put water in the small glass vase she'd brought from the Vicarage, before taking a pair of scissors from her bag and going into the garden.

'Lovely day,' said Ted Jackson, appearing from nowhere. 'Another heatwave coming, they reckon.'

'Well, we can always hope,' Tavy returned, making for a bed of early roses in an array of colours from soft blush to crimson, and snipping a few buds.

'Cheering the old place up, even when there's no furni-ture?'

In spite of herself, Tavy found she was glancing up at the first floor windows. 'Not all the rooms are empty,' she said.

'Upstairs, maybe.' He paused. 'You were working late last night?'

'Well, yes.'

He nodded. 'Jim forgot his tea flask and when he came back for it, he saw lights.' His smile was almost cherubic. 'He wondered, but I told him it must be that.'

Tavy moved unwarily and felt a thorn pierce her finger.

'Yes,' she said, sucking away the welling blood. 'That's what it was.'

Ted nodded. 'Nasty—them thorns,' he observed as he moved away. 'You want to take more care, Miss Tavy.'

Damn and double damn, thought Tavy as she went back to the house. Clearly, at some point, Jim had been an unseen spectator at the dining room window.

Not that there'd been anything untoward for him to see, she reminded herself hastily. And, hopefully, Barbie's arrival would provide a more fruitful topic for the rumour-mongers. But she would indeed have to take more care. In all sorts of ways.

She arranged the rosebuds in her vase and took it to Barbie's room, placing it on the bedside table.

'Ready and waiting,' she said under her breath as she turned away. 'So please make it soon—for both our sakes.'

But, suddenly, it was the weekend again, the roses had died and been replaced with still no sign of the missing lady.

And when she'd mentioned this to Jago, he'd said, apparently unperturbed, that Barbie would turn up when she saw fit, and not before.

He hadn't been back to the house, but, instead, he'd taken to calling her at six each evening for a progress report.

And she was shocked to find how soon she'd adjusted to this, even glancing at her watch, feeling her heartbeat quicken as the hour approached. On tenterhooks if his call

was a few minutes late. Struggling to appear cool and businesslike when the sound of his voice made her shake inside.

Fortunately, there was always plenty to tell him of a totally impersonal nature. The beautiful wooden floors in the
drawing room and dining room had been cleaned, restored
and polished until they glowed, redecoration was about to
begin and measurements had been taken for the curtains.
The pipe work for the new bathroom was also making good
progress.

Yet, each time Tavy switched off the phone, she found
herself caught in some limbo between misery and anger at
her own weakness.

Dinner at the Grange had been a bad mistake. But the picnic, on reflection, was a worse one, because she was already
being asked pointedly in the village how the job was going,
and if she was enjoying it, so word had clearly got around,
and she could afford no more such errors.

Especially when twice recently, she'd gone into the village shop to replenish the supplies of milk and teabags only
to find all conversation ceasing abruptly at her entrance.

Although they could simply be discussing the parish
meeting her father had called for the following Wednesday
evening, when the Archdeacon would be coming to speak
about the projected closure of Holy Trinity, and not wish to
mention it in front of her.

The surveyor's letter received three days before had been
frankly pessimistic, giving a ball-park figure of two hundred
thousand pounds minimum for repairs to the tower, and the
fabric of the rest of the building, including the roof.

'I think,' Mr Denison had said sadly, 'that this is what
they call a death warrant.'

And the Archdeacon's phone call had confirmed his view.

Since then, Tavy and her father had been busy posting
notices about the meeting all round the village, and Tavy

had spent an evening delivering copies of an explanatory newsletter to every household.

Tavy had hoped for an immediate groundswell of protest against the projected closure, but the response had been frankly muted. Strange, she thought, in view of the size of the congregation Holy Trinity attracted each Sunday. Perhaps they'd been shocked into silence.

But she too was in for a surprise. When she got back to the Vicarage on Thursday evening, a little abstracted because, for the first time, there had been no call from Jago, it was to find her father packing a small travel bag.

'I'm going away for a couple of days,' he said. 'To stay with Derek Castleton, an old friend from University days. I'm sure you've heard your mother and me talking about him. He was best man at our wedding.'

Tavy frowned. 'Is he the one who's been abroad on the missions?'

'Very much so, but he and his wife have been back for a couple of years now, and living in Milcaster.' He fastened the zip on his bag. 'We got back in touch, and I've been telling him about the difficult times Holy Trinity is facing. He's asked me over to discuss the matter.'

'Do you think he can suggest an answer?' Tavy asked hopefully.

Mr Denison paused. 'Perhaps.' His tone was odd. 'We shall just have to…wait and see.' He dropped a kiss on her hair. 'You'll be all right, darling, here on your own? I'll be back some time on Saturday. If there are any emergencies, Chris Fleming at Gunslade has agreed to help out.'

'Everything will be fine,' she assured him. 'I'll do girly things and watch daft programmes on television.'

'You'll be spoiled for choice,' the Vicar said drily as he left.

The sound of the car had barely died away when the phone rang.

'I'm afraid Mr Denison has been called away,' she rehearsed silently as she picked up the receiver and gave the Vicarage number.

'Octavia.' The low-pitched, husky voice was unmistakable, and, in spite of herself, her heart lurched in excitement. 'Sorry I couldn't ring before. I was delayed.'

'It doesn't matter,' she said, adding hurriedly, 'After all, you don't have to phone me each evening.'

'Oh, I think I do,' Jago said softly, and paused. 'How else would I know how the house was progressing?' His tone became brisker. 'But there's going to be a change of plan tomorrow. I've heard about a table and chairs in a country house sale about thirty miles away.

'I suggest we drive over in the morning to see them, and, if we like them, stay on and bid for them in the afternoon.'

'But it's your dining room and your furniture,' she said, stumbling a little. 'There's no reason to involve me.'

'Let's agree to differ,' he said briskly. 'I'll pick you up from Ladysmere at eleven.' He added, 'Boss's orders.'

And he was gone, leaving Tavy to catch her breath.

During her solitary supper and afterwards, she tried to work on her resentment at his arrogant and domineering ways, but all in vain. Because running through her head like a refrain were the words, 'I shall see him tomorrow. I shall be with him tomorrow.'

And the sheer absurdity of that made her cringe inwardly.

'I think I really have gone mad,' she whispered. 'But it won't last, and very soon I'll stop building cloud castles and be the sane and sensible Octavia Denison again.'

The following morning, in keeping with that resolve, she retrieved from her wardrobe the anonymous grey skirt she used to wear at Greenbrook School, teaming it with a short-sleeved white cotton blouse, and pinning her hair in a loose knot on top of her head, in acknowledgement of the fact that the temperature was climbing again.

Once at work, there was no time for brooding as the
shower for Jago's private bathroom had been delivered without several essential components. There was also a sheaf
of estimates from the decorator to check and print off, and
the curtain fitter who'd arrived punctually at nine o'clock
to measure the windows in the drawing room, dining room
and master bedroom, was clearly disappointed to be dealing
with Tavy rather than the new owner himself.

'I was really looking forward to meeting him,' she said
petulantly as she descended from her stepladder. 'Of course,
like everyone else, I'm such a fan.'

'Of course,' Tavy echoed politely.

The people's choice also arrived punctually, cool in dark
jeans, a faded indigo shirt, and sunglasses.

He looked her over, his brows lifting, as his gaze lingered
on her hair. 'Very businesslike.'

'Because this is business,' Tavy returned crisply. 'My
time off starts tomorrow.'

His mouth slanted into a grin. 'I'll consider myself rebuked.'

Tavy was aware of Ted Jackson watching as she got into
the Jeep.

Putting two and two together to make five and then some,
she thought biting her lip. I wish I'd borrowed Dad's brief-
case as a finishing touch.

But the drive through lanes, their verges heavy with
Queen Anne's lace, while the lightest of winds ruffled the
long grasses, soon eased much of her tension, even if it made
her wish that she'd left her hair loose for the breeze.

Ashingham Hall, where the sale was being held, was
rather like Ladysmere—a hotchpotch of various styles,
which, according to Jago, had been sold to a company offering upmarket residential care for the elderly.

The furniture to be auctioned was being displayed *in situ*
but, instead of making straight for the dining room, Jago

wandered from room to room making notes in his catalogue, with Tavy getting more and more bewildered as she followed him.

At last: 'But you can't possibly want that,' she whispered to him urgently. 'It's a Victorian whatnot and totally hideous. I thought you came for a table.'

'I did,' he returned softly. 'But it's unwise to appear too keen when there are dealers around.'

Accordingly when they reached the dining room, Tavy struggled to keep her face straight as Jago stood in rapt admiration of an ornately framed oil painting of some gloomy cattle grazing in an improbable Scottish glen.

'Getting inspiration for your own work?' she enquired dulcetly.

'Now, how could I ever hope to emulate that?' he asked and turned, at last, to look at the table.

It was the best thing they'd seen so far, a large circle of elegant walnut on a carved pedestal base, with one extra leaf and eight matching chairs.

Tavy had to stifle a gasp of pleasure, and saw that Jago too had allowed himself a swift smile of satisfaction.

Aware they were being observed by a sharp-faced man, his catalogue pushed into a pocket in his linen jacket, Tavy moved closer to Jago. She said in a clear, carrying voice, 'It's all right, but we want a refectory table, darling, and a couple of those big chairs with arms for each end of it. You promised me.'

Jago leered at her. 'Don't fancy me as King Arthur, then, doll? Come on. Perhaps I'll have more luck with you up in the bedrooms.'

When they reached the main hall, Tavy tried to hang back, but Jago's hand was firm under her arm, guiding her away from the broad flight of stairs and back to the entrance.

'No need to panic,' he advised coolly. 'My sleeping arrangements are already catered for.'

Tavy lifted her chin. 'I hadn't forgotten,' she said, wondering how many more flowers she would throw away before the elusive Barbie made an appearance.

'Apparently there's a good pub in the village,' Jago went on. 'Let's get an early lunch, and then we'll go back for a chat with the auctioneer.'

Other people had the same idea about lunch, but Jago and Tavy managed to snaffle the last parasol shaded table on a terrace overlooking a small river, where ducks foraged busily and moorhens played hide-and-seek under the drooping pale green fronds of a willow tree.

They ordered a Ploughman's Platter which came with generous slices of ham, two kinds of pâté, three sorts of cheese and a green salad, all accompanied by a tray of small dishes holding pickles and chutneys, butter in a cooling dish and crusty bread, still warm from the oven. With it, they drank clear, cold cider.

She said, 'The girl at the end table keeps looking at you and whispering to her mother. I think you've been recognised.'

He sighed. 'Even wearing the shades?'

She nodded. 'Even so, you're fairly unmistakable.'

'Present company excepted, of course,' he said. 'The first time we met, you hadn't a clue who I was.'

She looked back at the river, remembering the coolness of water against her bare skin and felt the swift, urgent clench of her body. She said quickly, 'I just wanted you to go.'

He said quietly, 'Whereas I wanted equally badly to stay.'

There was a catch in her voice. 'Please—don't say things like that.'

'Why? Don't you like to be thought desirable? Or has that idiot Patrick Wilding given you a complex?'

She swallowed. 'You can hardly claim any high moral ground. He was already spoken for. So are you.' She added, 'If you recall.'

'I have no intention of forgetting.' He went on, musingly, '"Spoken for". What a sweet old-fashioned phrase.'

'I'm an old-fashioned girl,' she said. 'If not particularly sweet. And your fan is coming over.'

She watched as Jago turned smilingly to greet the girl, who was young, awestruck, and extremely pretty. She'd brought one of the pub's white paper napkins with her and shyly asked him to sign it.

'I can do better than that.' He took the pen she was offering. 'Stand quite still.'

He studied her blushing face for a moment, then proceeded to draw on the napkin with swift, assured strokes.

'What's your name?' he asked as he finished.

She told him, 'Verity,' and he wrote it under the instant likeness he'd achieved before signing his own name and adding the date.

As the girl ran back beaming to her family, Tavy said, 'That was a nice thing to do. She'll love you for ever.'

'I'm capable of the odd, kindly gesture.' He signalled to the waitress to bring the bill. 'Now, shall we be getting back—in case I get besieged by potential lovers and miss out on my dining table?'

His mood had suddenly changed, she thought in bewilderment, and not simply because other people were turning to look at him, murmuring to each other.

Back to business, she told herself, reaching for her bag. Which was, after all, the real purpose of her presence here. And certainly gave her no reason to feel quite so desperately forlorn, or have to struggle so hard to hide it.

CHAPTER ELEVEN

IT WAS GETTING on for late afternoon as they drove back to Hazelton Magna. The auctioneer had taken his time over the sale and, understandably, had kept the best lots until last.

Tavy was glad to see that the hideous whatnot failed to reach its reserve, and the glum Scottish cattle went for a tenner, probably, as Jago said, for the frame.

When the walnut table and chairs finally came up for sale, and hands were raised round the room, Tavy nudged him. 'Aren't you going to bid?' she whispered.

He shook his head. 'The auctioneer's doing that for me, on commission.'

'That man who was watching us—he wants them too.'

'Only if he can make a profit on resale,' Jago returned softly. 'Whereas I'm buying them for myself.'

'But he'll force up the price,' she said. 'You must have set a limit.'

'I'll pay whatever I have to,' he said. 'For something I really want.' The tawny eyes rested on her ironically. 'Don't you know that yet, Octavia?'

She stared down at her catalogue. She said very quietly, 'I don't think I know you at all.'

In the end, Jago got his furniture with comparative ease, the dealer in the linen jacket clearly deciding it was a battle he couldn't win.

'And it will all be delivered on Monday,' Jago said with satisfaction as they turned up Ladysmere's drive.

Tavy glanced at him. 'You sound as if Christmas is coming early.'

'The house is beginning to come together,' he said. 'It's a good feeling.'

She said sedately, 'I hope Barbie will be equally pleased—when she arrives.'

'It should be any day now.' He parked outside the main entrance and switched off the engine, turning to face her. 'She seems to fascinate you,' he remarked. 'Why don't you ask me about her?'

Tavy shrugged defensively, 'Because she has nothing to do with me.' *And because I don't want to risk hearing the answer.*

She went on, 'I wouldn't want her to find another vase of dead roses, that's all.'

'Is it?' There was an odd intensity in his voice. 'Is it really all, Octavia.'

'Yes,' she said with curt emphasis. She reached for the door handle. 'And I'm sure you have somewhere else to be, so I'll see everyone on their way and lock up.'

'We'll both do it,' he said. 'Then I'll drive you home.' Adding, as her lips parted, 'And no argument.'

She drew a deep breath. She said stonily, 'Just as you wish.'

His grin was unforgivable. 'If only that were true,' he said, and swung himself lithely out of the Jeep.

Once inside, Tavy found there were emails and phone messages to deal with, enabling her to regain her composure.

I shouldn't get lured into that kind of exchange, she thought, feeling that slow ache of wretchedness building inside her once again. *It's stupid and futile, and I'm simply making myself unhappy, when I have neither the right nor the reason to feel anything of the kind.*

Or to hope. Only—to remember.

And, in spite of herself, her hand lifted and her fingers touched her trembling mouth.

The workmen departed, and Tavy made her rounds to check that the house was secure for the weekend, moving deliberately slowly, in the hope that Jago might eventually tire of waiting and go on his way.

But no such luck, because, when she emerged, he was leaning against the Jeep, talking to Ted Jackson, their faces serious and preoccupied.

As she hesitated, Ted lifted a hand in farewell and walked off to his van.

As Tavy got into the Jeep and fastened her seat belt, Jago said abruptly, 'Why didn't you tell me?'

'Tell you what?'

That I've committed the ultimate, disastrous folly by fall- ing in love with you? That every minute of every hour I spend with you is an unflagging battle to hide it, especially when you smile and flirt with me, because nothing in my life has taught me to deal with this situation. Except that I know the pain of being away from you would be even worse.

And the most scaring thing of all is that whenever we're alone, I think of your mouth—your hands—touching me. Possessing me. Taking me for ever. While, when we're apart, you fill my dreams in ways I never imagined.

He'd turned in his seat and was staring at her. 'About next Wednesday's meeting with the Archdeacon. Ted says there are notices all over the village, yet you haven't said a word.'

'But you aren't here during the week.'

'Not usually,' he said. 'But next Wednesday I shall make a point of it. Like it or not, I'm coming to live here, Octavia, and the parish church is an important part of village life. Of course I want to be involved in a discussion over its fate.' He added crisply, 'For your father's sake, if for no other reason. I'll have a word with him presently, when I drop you off at the Vicarage.'

'He's away,' said Tavy, and could have bitten out her tongue.

'When will he be back?'

'Some time tomorrow,' she returned reluctantly. 'He—he's visiting an old friend. Someone who might be able to help.'

'Occasionally new friends can be just as useful.' He paused. 'I'm really sorry, Octavia. It explains why you've been so quiet—so withdrawn today. You must be worried sick.'

She stiffened. 'Withdrawn? I wasn't aware of it.'

'No,' he said, tight-lipped. 'Probably not.' And started the Jeep's engine.

When they reached the Vicarage, she said quickly, 'You can drop me here at the gate.'

'I could also drop you into a fast-flowing river,' he drawled, easing the Jeep up the drive. 'Don't think it hasn't occurred to me.'

Tavy sat back mutinously. I should offer him coffee, she thought, but I'm not going to. I shall simply thank him for a pleasant day, go in and shut the door. Firmly.

Then the door in question came into view, and she leaned forward with a gasp of pure horror.

Because splashed across its dark wood in white paint were the words 'BITCH' and 'SLAG' in large uneven letters, while one of the glass panels at the top of the door now bore a gaping hole.

'Dear God,' said Jago, and brought the Jeep to an abrupt halt. 'Stay there,' he directed, jumping out.

She obeyed, largely because she was shaking too much to do otherwise. The ugly words seemed to be swimming in front of her eyes. Accusing her...

But why?

Jago came back, looking grim. 'No one about,' he said. 'But I guess your own paint was used.'

'Why?'

'Because the garage door's wide open, and the paint pot and brush have been thrown inside. They'd probably yield some interesting fingerprints, if you involved the police. Do you want to?'

She said hoarsely, 'No. It—it must be vandals.'

His mouth twisted. 'If you say so. However, the paint's emulsion and still damp. If we're quick, it might scrub off the door with hot water, some household cleaner and a stiff brush. Anyway, I can try.'

He came round to her side and opened the door. 'Here, give me your hand, and your keys. I'll have a go at the paint, but I can't do much about the broken pane. Although, I could ring Ted Jackson. I bet among his friends and relations there's a glazier prepared to turn out in an emergency.'

'No,' she said quickly. 'No, I don't want him—or anybody in the village—to know about this. I'll find someone in *Yellow Pages* tomorrow.'

Jago took her to the door and unlocked it, steering her carefully past the scatter of broken shards in the hall and the heavy stone responsible.

He said brusquely, 'Go and sit down, while I clean up. You're as white as a sheet.' He paused. 'Does your father have any brandy?'

She nodded. 'On top of the bookcase in his study.' Her voice shook. 'He keeps it for parishioners who've had a shock, or are in some kind of trouble.'

He spoke more gently. 'Then you definitely qualify on one count, if not two.' He lifted her into his arms before she had time to protest and carried her into the sitting room, placing her on the sofa. 'Now, stay there while I attend to everything.'

She leaned back against the cushions, still hardly able to

believe what had happened. Trying almost desperately to make sense of it.

When Jago came back with the brandy, she said, 'You don't believe it's hooligans. You think it's Patrick, don't you?'

He looked surprised. 'Actually, no. He might shout and bluster, but this is sheer spite.' His mouth tightened. 'No, I have another candidate in mind.'

She grimaced over the brandy, but she could feel it dissolving the cold, numb feeling inside her. 'I suppose you mean Fiona. But why?'

'Because she's just suffered a serious disappointment, and is lashing out because of it. Although she's not alone in that.'

About to take another sip, she sat up instead, her eyes widening. 'What's happened? Have she and Patrick split up?'

He said coldly, 'I neither know nor care. But would it necessarily be such a bad thing, if so?'

'Yes.'

'For God's sake,' he said wearily. 'We're not talking about some latter-day Romeo and Juliet here, but a couple of worthless cheats. If you remember.'

'In other words, they'd be better off without each other.' She took a deep breath. 'That's what people always say, isn't it. But they forget something important.'

'Which is?'

She said in a low voice, staring down at her brandy, 'That you can't help loving the wrong person. It happens, and it makes no difference to know that it's totally one-sided, or that it could never work in a million years anyway, and that you'll simply end up more lonely and more unhappy than you ever dreamed possible.'

She stopped abruptly, not daring to look up, scared that she had revealed too much. Even, heaven help her, given herself away.

There was a silence, then he said sardonically, 'I bow to your superior wisdom in matters of the heart, Octavia, although perhaps wisdom isn't the exact term. Now, excuse me please, while I attend to more practical matters.'

At the door, he paused, 'By the way, that's a good cognac you have there, so try not to treat it like medicine, but as yet another of life's pleasurable experiences that has so far passed you by.'

Leaving her clutching the glass and gasping with indignation. Which somehow turned out to be a better cure for feeling forlorn, shaky and victimised than any amount of brandy.

How dared he just—throw in a reference to her undoubted innocence like that? Because that's what he'd meant by that last remark.

Besides, what if she was still a virgin? That was no one's business but her own. And would continue to be so until some time in the future, when she'd recovered her senses, stopped crying for the moon, and met someone decent, honourable and caring. Someone who'd be glad that she'd kept herself for him.

Not, she thought wryly, that she'd had much choice in the matter so far. Patrick hadn't wanted her, and as for Jago…

He'd just been amusing himself. She'd always known that. Testing the water, no doubt, with the kisses that she was unable to forget, and the shaming sensations that their memory aroused.

What she must do now was behave as if the implication in his parting words had simply—passed her by. Be grateful for his help, but stay on the cool side of friendly. That was the safe—the only—thing to do.

She took another sip, felt the healing warmth spread, and decided if brandy was an acquired taste, she might just have made the acquisition.

She lay back, closing her eyes, and letting her thoughts drift. Fiona Culham, who'd once derided her as a skinny redhead, to come here, paint insults on the Vicarage door and smash one of its panes? It almost defied belief.

Almost…

Because she found herself reluctantly remembering Fiona's visit to Ladysmere, and the thinly veiled threat she'd uttered in parting.

But I haven't talked to anyone about her—or Patrick, she whispered silently. In fact I've barely given them a thought.

And she can't be suffering from a belated attack of jealousy—not when Patrick was only pretending to date me, and on her instructions.

None of it made any sense, she thought wearily. But that didn't make it any less disturbing or unpleasant.

She finished the brandy and rose to take the glass to the kitchen. The front door was shut, when she went out into the hall, but she could hear the sound of a scrubbing brush being vigorously employed outside. And there was a dustpan and brush at the side of the mat, containing fragments of glass.

In the kitchen, the doors of the cupboards under the sink had been left standing wide, just as if her father had been there rummaging for something, and the realisation took her by the throat with an almost terrifying tenderness.

She took a bottle of beer from the fridge, uncapped it, and went out of the back door, round the side of the house to where Jago was working.

He had stripped off his shirt and draped it over a bush, and the late sun made his skin look burnished. The dark shadowing of hair on his chest tapered into a thin line, which disappeared under the waistband of his pants.

He turned to smile at her. 'Ah,' he said. 'From project manager to lifesaver.' He took the beer, and she watched the muscles move in his strong throat as he took a first deep swallow.

She was thirsty too, she realised with shock. Parched for him. And starving.

Afraid of self-betrayal, she hurried into speech. 'You've done a terrific job. The paint's nearly gone.'

Jago gave his efforts a disparaging look. 'The lettering maybe, but the woodwork's still badly stained. It's going to need professional attention.'

She forced a smile. 'Well, after next Wednesday, it won't be our problem any more.'

He sat down on the step, and drank some more beer. 'Things might turn out better than you think,' he suggested.

'I'm sure the hierarchy has already made up its mind.' She looked determinedly back at the door. 'I'm so grateful for this, but I really mustn't keep you any longer. You've spent far too much time on it already.'

'If that's a pointed hint for me to leave,' Jago said cordially. 'Forget it. Because I'm going nowhere.'

Her head jerked round. 'What are you talking about?'

'I'm not letting you spend the night alone. We can stay here or we can go to Barkland Grange. I'd opt for here, because of the damage to the door, and in case your visitor should return, but it's your decision.'

She said, her voice shaking, 'You sound as if you've already decided for me. But it's quite ridiculous. You can't really believe anyone will come back.'

'Probably not,' he said. 'I only know I'm not taking the chance. And that your father wouldn't want me to.'

The killer blow, thought Tavy.

She glared at him mutinously. 'How many times do I have to tell you—both of you, for that matter—that I'm not a child?'

'Well, when I'm convinced,' he said. 'I'll let you know.' Adding unforgivably, 'And sulking does not help your cause, my sweet.'

He paused, then said more gently, 'Do you really want to spend the night with your head under the covers, Octavia, jumping at every strange noise, yet too scared to go downstairs and check them out?' His sudden grin was coaxing. 'Wouldn't it be easier just to settle for the sound of my snoring?'

'I don't know.' She bit her lip, trying not to smile back. 'Do you snore?'

'I haven't the faintest idea, but I could obtain references.'

She winced inwardly, but kept her voice light. 'Maybe I'll just put cotton wool in my ears.'

'Good thinking.' Jago finished his beer and rose. 'As regards food, there's a good Indian place in Market Tranton that delivers. I suggest that when I've finished here and showered, we order in, and spend a quiet evening watching television.'

'You actually think someone's going to bring us curry all that way?' Tavy shook her head, resolutely turning her mind from unwelcome images of Jago in the shower. 'Never in a million years.'

'Want to bet?' He studied her for a moment. 'If I win, you change out of that business garb into something a little more appealing.'

She swallowed. 'And if I win?'

He said softly, 'Then you can name your own price—except, of course, sending me on my way.'

Just as the ensuing silence between them began to stretch out into tingling eternity, she heard herself say huskily, 'Except, of course, I'm not a gambler. Therefore I'll have chicken biriyani with naan bread.'

Then turned and went back the way she'd come.

In the end, in spite of herself, she did change into a floral cotton dress which was, quite deliberately, neither new nor particularly exciting. And that was probably Jago's estimation too, because when he came into the kitchen after telephoning the curry house, barefoot, his dark hair gleaming damply and his shirt hanging open over his stained and grubby pants, he glanced at her but said nothing.

As she began to set the kitchen table, she said huskily, 'I've been trying to figure out what to say to Dad about the door.' She shrugged almost helplessly. 'He's got so much on his mind, I don't want to give him further worries.'

'For all that, I think you have to tell him the truth, Octavia.' His tone was level. 'He has a right to know.'

'But it would hurt him terribly—to know someone disliked me enough to do such a thing.'

He said meditatively, 'Someone once said that to be hated by certain people should be regarded as a compliment. I think he had a point.'

She sighed. 'Perhaps, but I doubt if Dad will see it like that.' She paused. 'Thank you for blocking up the hole in the glass, by the way. I'll try and get it properly fixed in the morning.'

He nodded. 'Everything will seem better tomorrow.'

Supper was delicious, starting with poppadums accompanied by relishes in little pots, and proceeding to Tavy's beautifully spiced biriyani with its exotic vegetable curry and Jago's lamb balti and pilau rice, with cans of light beer to wash it all down.

As they cleared away, Tavy said lightly, 'After all this alcohol, I'd better have my coffee black.'

He grinned at her. 'Then I can't tempt you to some more cognac?'

You could probably tempt me to walk with you to the gates of hell. The thought came unbidden and was instantly pushed away.

She reached down to empty the sink, keeping her face averted to conceal her rising colour. 'Not unless you want me to fall asleep in front of the television.' That struck the right note—jokey and casual. Now all she had to do was keep it that way. Until bedtime, anyway…

It was easier than she thought. She wasn't a great television fan, and neither was Mr Denison who confined his interest to sport, and the occasional classic serial.

But Jago found a channel showing a recent hit production of *HMS Pinafore* and she settled down on the sofa opposite to his and revelled in Gilbert and Sullivan's glorious absurdities.

At the interval, she said hesitantly, 'You must find this very dull.'

'On the contrary. I'll have you know I was raised on Gilbert and Sullivan,' Jago retorted, walking across to draw the curtains. 'Dad was a leading light with the local operatic society, and I even had a couple of walk-ons in the chorus myself.'

She shook her head as she lit the lamps standing on small tables behind the sofas. 'I can't imagine it.'

His brows lifted. 'You think I was born with a guitar in one hand and some groupie in the other? Not a bit of it. Any more than your father came into the world in a clerical collar, clutching a Bible.'

'That's certainly true.' She smiled reminiscently. 'My mother told me that when they first met, he was one of the lads. And yet she wasn't really surprised when he told her he was going to be ordained.'

'No.' He looked up at the photograph on the mantelpiece and she remembered finding him studying it on his first visit to the Vicarage. 'I don't suppose she was easily fazed.' He paused. 'What did she want for you, Octavia?'

She said slowly, 'We never really discussed it, although I know she was pleased when I got my place at University. I suppose she thought, as I did, that we'd have plenty of time to talk as friends, and not just mother and daughter.'

His voice was quiet. 'It should have happened.'

Then the music began for Act Two, and Tavy, her throat tightening uncontrollably, hurriedly turned her attention back to romantic and class entanglements in the Royal Navy, and their preposterous but delightful resolution.

When it was over, she turned to him, smiling. 'That was lovely. Just what I needed.' She glanced at her watch and hesitated. 'I usually have hot chocolate at this time of night. Would you…?'

'No, thanks,' he said. 'The nanny I mentioned believed in milky drinks at bedtime. They always seemed to have skin on them, and it's taken me years to escape from their memory.'

She said, 'Then I'll see about your room…'

'Not necessary.' He indicated the sofa he'd been occupying. 'I'll sleep here. Just a blanket and a pillow will be fine.'

'But making up the spare bed would be no trouble.'

He said gently, but very definitely, 'However, I'd prefer to stay down here. I'll probably watch American cop shows for a while.'

'Yes,' she said, slowly. 'Of course. Just as you wish.'

She went up to the spare room, took the thin quilt and a pillow from the bed, and carried them down to the sitting room.

Jago had turned off one of the lamps and the whole room seemed to have shrunk to the small oval illumined by the other. It was something that must have happened a thousand times before, Tavy thought, but never with this kind of disturbing intimacy.

She said quickly, 'Are you sure you'll be all right like this. Is there anything else I can get you?'

'Not a thing. It's all fine.' His smile was swift. Almost perfunctory. 'Now go and get a good night's sleep. And stop worrying.'

She left closing the door behind her, and went to the kitchen. She set a pan on the hob, got the milk from the fridge and took down the tin of chocolate powder from its shelf.

Then stood, staring at them, aware of the passage of time only by the heavy beat of her pulses.

It occurred to her that she had not been completely honest with Jago just now, when she said she had not discussed her future with her mother.

She remembered asking her once if she had always planned to be a Vicar's wife, and Mrs Denison's soft, joyous burst of laughter.

'No, it was the last thing in the world I had in mind,' she'd returned frankly. 'And a commitment everyone said I should consider long and hard. But you see, darling, I knew from the first your father was the only man I ever would love and my wish to spend my life with him outweighed anything else.

'And that's the kind of certainty I hope for you, Tavy,' she added seriously. 'For you to meet someone and know that you want to belong to him alone, for ever. Don't settle for anything less, my dearest.'

Tavy put everything neatly back in its place, switched off the light and crossed to the stairs, certain at last about what she was going to do.

Him alone, said the heat in her blood and the fever in her mind. *Him alone—even though it can't be for ever. Even if it's just one night...*

CHAPTER TWELVE

WHILE HER BATH was running, she searched through her dressing table for the slim package she had hidden there so long ago. It was at the very back of the bottom drawer, and she retrieved it, removing its tissue-paper wrappings with gentle hands, and shaking out the contents.

It was the summer dressing gown that her mother had given her before she left for university, white lawn embroidered with tiny golden flowers and dark green leaves. Such a pretty thing and never worn.

Or not until now...

She held it against her as she looked in the mirror. Wondered what he would think when he saw her.

Wondered too, as she turned away, what her mother's reaction would be if she knew what she was planning? Shock? Certainly—and disappointment too.

Yet suppose you'd fallen in love with the wrong man, and knew that any relationship would be totally one-sided and doomed to heartbreak. What then? she thought, sliding down into the warm water. Would you tell me to walk away, and forget him?

Because I would say—I can't. That I need at least one precious memory to go with me wherever the future takes me.

And nothing else can be allowed to matter.

Him alone...

She dried herself, and put on the robe, tying the sash

tightly round her slender waist. She loosened her hair and brushed it until it shone. Then she took one last look in the mirror at the pale girl, staring back at her, her lips parted and eyes bright with nerves, because she would have to rely on instinct rather than experience in the hours ahead of her.

The girl she no longer wished to be, she thought, her bare feet making no sound on the stairs as she descended to the hall.

He wasn't watching television. The room was in darkness, but as she pushed the door wider, the lamp by his sofa came on, and he sat up, the quilt falling away from his body as he stared at her.

He said sharply, 'What's the matter? Did you hear someone? Something?'

'No.'

'Then why are you here?'

Upstairs it had all seemed so simple. He might not love her, but he wanted her. His kisses had told her that, even if he hadn't kissed her for quite some time.

She said huskily, 'I can't sleep. I don't like being alone.' She searched the dark face, the narrowed tawny eyes for some response, and swallowed. 'Jago—I—I want you to be with me—please.'

She stared down at the carpet and waited in a silence that seemed to stretch into for ever.

And when he eventually spoke, his voice was light, almost amused.

'In that case, sweetheart, take off that pretty piece of nonsense you're wearing and come here.'

Her head jerked up in disbelief. He was leaning back against his pillow, arms folded across his bare chest. The faint smile curling the corners of his mouth said nothing of desire. Even the uttered endearment had been casual, almost mocking.

She said, 'I don't understand...'

'It's quite simple,' Jago drawled. 'It seems we're about to have an intimate encounter which I want to begin with the pleasure of seeing you naked. Therefore…' His hand moved in a gesture of explicit and sensual command.

But this isn't how it's meant to be. The words shivered through her brain. It can't be…

She'd imagined he would come to her, take her in his arms. That she would bury her face rapturously in the satin of his skin, breathing the scent of him, the taste of him before offering her mouth to his kiss, and her body for his undressing.

That she would welcome with eagerness the exploration of his eyes—his hands—his mouth—her own shyness and uncertainty lost in the glory of their unstinted mutuality.

Something, she realised, her throat tightening painfully, that did not exist outside her imagination.

And, at the same time, she knew that she could never do as he required. Could not just strip—and have him look at her as if judging whether or not she warranted his time and attention.

Told herself that if she mattered to him at all, he would never ask such a thing of her.

'Having second thoughts?' His harsh query held a jeering note. 'How very wise. Because, understand this, Octavia. I'm not your comfort blanket, nor your consolation prize.'

He added, 'And whatever you may choose to believe, I'm here tonight only to ride shotgun, not to exploit the situation by using you for a few hours of casual sex.

'And if you were thinking straight, you'd be grateful to me, because that's not how it ought to be when it's your first time with a man. It should actually mean something.'

She closed her eyes, standing rigid under the shock of his rejection. Her voice trembled. 'Will you—*please*—stop treating me like a child?'

'On the contrary,' he said. 'It's a damned sight safer than

treating you like a woman. Now go back to your room, and let's both try and get some rest for the remainder of this eternally bloody night.'

It was over. And there was nothing more to say or do. She had made a terrible, sickening mistake.

Now, all that was left for her was to get out—get away from him—with some few shreds of dignity. Walking steadily out of the room without hurrying, or stumbling over the hem of her robe.

As she closed the door behind her, she heard the faint click as he switched off the lamp, and the creak of the sofa as he turned over, composing himself for sleep again after that brief, unwelcome interruption.

And she felt the first hot wave of humiliation sweep over her, before gathering the skirt of her robe in one fist, and pressing the other against her shaking mouth, she fled up the stairs, back to the darkness and silence that waited for her there.

She did not allow herself to cry. Tears were an indulgence that her stupidity did not deserve.

She dropped the robe to the carpet and slid into bed, shivering as the chill of the sheets met her heated flesh, and burying her face in the pillow, in a futile longing to blot out the whole of the last half hour.

What in the world had possessed her to forget every principle she'd ever believed in and throw herself at him like that?

Because he'd never wanted her—not seriously. And particularly not when Barbie was coming back into his life. His kisses had been no more than a conditioned reflex response to a female presence, but one he was well able to control.

His casual reference to Fiona Culham should have warned her, and it was no consolation to know that Fiona too had offered herself without success.

Oh, why the hell had she spoken to him? she wailed silently. If she'd just stood there in silence waiting for him to make the first move, she might have managed some ludicrous pretence that she was sleepwalking.

He wouldn't have believed her—that was too much to hope—but at least she'd have spared herself his refusal of her stammering offer, and been able to make a face-saving exit.

Whereas now...

The thought of having to face him in the morning made her feel cold all over. And empty too, as if everything joyous and hopeful had withered and died inside her.

The probability of leaving Hazelton Magna no longer seemed a disaster but a kind of practical salvation. She would have to stop working for him, of course. And moving from the village provided her with a feasible excuse for the world at large.

Although it meant, she realised with aching wistfulness, that she would never see the work on Ladysmere completed, and the place reborn in all its new glory.

On the plus side, she would not have to witness him living there with Barbie, she thought, pushing herself into the mattress as if hoping it would open and swallow her, never to be seen again.

But at least she hadn't committed the ultimate folly of telling him she loved him, and she would have to be eternally grateful for that.

Let him think it was a mixture of sexual curiosity and a need for reassurance that had driven her to seek him out. Still embarrassing but not terminal.

Which, under the circumstances, was as much as she could hope for. And if her heart was breaking, at least he would never know.

Her eyes felt as if she'd rubbed them with grit, when she opened them to another sun-filled morning.

Not surprisingly, she had slept badly, but she had also

slept late, and she could only hope that by this time Jago would have removed himself from the Vicarage.

But the sound of the shower running in the bathroom told her that she hoped in vain.

She washed at the old-fashioned basin in her room, and dragged on denim shorts and a white T-shirt before plaiting her hair into a thick braid and going downstairs.

In the sitting room, the quilt was neatly folded at one end of the sofa, with the pillow on top of it. Resolutely turning her back on this unwelcome reminder, Tavy pulled back the curtains, and opened the window, then went into the hall and, with a certain amount of trepidation, unfastened the front door.

It still looked messy, but there'd been no additions in the night, which was one relief, she thought, heading for the kitchen.

Be relaxed, be casual, she adjured herself as she spooned coffee into the percolator, and sliced bread for the toaster. But make it clear, if mentioned, that last night is a taboo subject.

As the kitchen door swung open behind her with its usual squeak, she braced herself and turned, hoping that her face did not betray her inner emotional turmoil and wretchedness.

But to her astonishment, it was not Jago but Patrick who stood there, looking daggers at her.

'So,' he said bitingly. 'I hope you're pleased with yourself.'

Never less so, she thought, but you, thank heaven, don't ever need to know that.

She lifted her chin. 'I didn't hear the doorbell.'

'Because I didn't ring it. I imagine you were expecting me.'

'No,' she said. 'Unless you've come to apologise for your girlfriend's act of vandalism.'

'In your dreams.' He walked to the kitchen table, spilling the contents of a manila envelope he was carrying across its surface. 'See these photographs?'

'She could hardly miss them,' Jago said from the doorway. He was wearing the dark jeans, his hair was damp and he was barefoot, moving silently as a cat as he came to Tavy's side.

'Brought your holiday snaps to show us, Patrick?' he asked affably. He picked up some of them, brows raised. 'A block of flats, rather than luxury apartments in the sun, I'd say. And there's Fiona leaving, and you on the doorstep kissing her goodbye in your bathrobe, of all things. Just a hint—do you think the world is ready for those legs?'

Patrick was crimson with anger as he made an unavailing grab for the photographs.

'You keep your bloody nose out,' he yelled. 'And what are you doing here anyway?'

Jago shrugged. 'After your girlfriend's performance yesterday, I decided Octavia needed some personal protection.'

'Oh, yes,' the other sneered. 'And we all know what that means, don't we?'

'It means I spent an uncomfortable night on the Vicarage sofa. Nothing else.'

'A likely bloody story.' Patrick swung round on Tavy. 'But you're going to be so sorry for this, you treacherous little bitch. Because you're not the only one who can take photographs.'

'What are you saying?' Tavy dropped the photo she was studying back on the table. 'That I had something to do with—this?' She shook her head. 'For God's sake, Patrick. I don't even have a camera.'

'You were there, sneaking about that Sunday morning.' He glared at her. 'Who else could it have been?'

'I imagine a professional with a zoom lens,' Jago drawled. 'One of the enquiry agents that Hugh Latimer has been using to report on his former wife's affairs. Or did you think such people never ventured out of London?' He tutted. 'Big mistake, Mr Wilding. One of many, I suspect.'

'You shut your bloody mouth, or I'll do it for you,' Patrick snarled.

'Inadvisable,' said Jago silkily. 'I work out. You don't.'

Tavy said shakily, 'Jago…no…please.'

The glance from the tawny eyes was hooded. His tone faintly brusque. 'Don't worry, Octavia. I won't do too much damage. He's probably bruised enough already.' He added critically, 'Although my old nanny would probably say he should have his mouth washed out.'

He looked contemptuously at Patrick. 'So, the great love affair died with Fiona's dreams of fortune. Did you really think it would survive—or that you were the only one in her extra-marital life?'

'What the hell do you know about it?'

'More than you, certainly,' Jago returned. 'Because Hugh Latimer tells me these weren't the only photographs of Fiona's fond farewells to be produced at the divorce settlement meeting, which explains why the negotiations stopped so abruptly, and so disastrously for her.

'Her lawyers backed away when they recognised among the usual suspects an important married client who would certainly not wish to be involved in a divorce.'

Patrick gave him a venomous look. 'You're lying.'

'In that case, tell me where she is,' said Jago quietly. 'And I'll rush round and apologise.' He paused, allowed the silence to lengthen, and nodded. 'My guess is that her work on the Vicarage front door was a parting shot on her way out of Hazelton Magna, leaving no forwarding address.'

'And who are you to take the moral high ground anyway, you womanising scum?' Patrick demanded. 'Have you told Little Miss Virtue here how your best mate had a complete mental breakdown after you went off with his wife? How the two of you have never spoken since you destroyed his marriage?'

He glanced at Tavy's stricken face and grinned unpleasantly. 'No, I thought not. Although, thanks to you, she's hardly the Vicar's untouched and untouchable daughter any longer so maybe she won't be too shocked.'

His smile widened. 'In fact, it's her father who has the nasty surprise coming to him. And it couldn't happen to a nicer family.'

He bundled up the photographs and went, pushing his way aggressively out of the kitchen. A few seconds later, they heard the front door slam.

'Ouch,' Jago remarked. 'That reminds me. We need to call a glazier. Shall we do that before or after coffee?'

She stared at him. 'You could do that? You could sit down and have breakfast—as if nothing had happened?'

He said coolly, 'I told you what was going to happen, Octavia. If it helps, I'm sorry to be proved right.' He paused. 'By the way, what was all that talk about unpleasant surprises?'

She gestured impatiently. 'Does it matter? Just Patrick hitting back, I suppose.' She added bitterly, 'Probably trying to hide that his heart's just been broken.'

'Ah, yes,' he said. 'But I'm sure it will mend quite quickly.'

She poured the coffee and brought it to the table. She said stonily, 'Unlike Pete Hilton's, apparently. And would you like a boiled egg?'

'That,' he said, 'was rather different. And, yes, four minutes, please.'

There was a silence, then he said, 'Aren't you going to ask me about my part in Pete's marriage break-up, and its aftermath?'

'No,' Tavy said, setting a pan of water to boil and taking the eggs from the crock. 'It's none of my business.'

As she set egg cups, plates and spoons on the table, Jago caught her hand. His voice was harsh and urgent. 'Is that all you have to say? Your usual bloody response?'

Now if ever was the time to ask. To say to him, 'Was your friend's wife called Barbie? Is this why you've chosen to bury yourself in the country, so that the newspapers won't find that she's with you again, and rake up the old scandal?'

But I can't ask, because I don't want to hear the answer, she thought. Because I may not be able to bear it.

She made herself shrug. Removed her hand from his clasp. 'What else is there to say? You have your life. I have mine. And I can't share your cavalier attitude to love, marriage and fidelity.'

She swallowed. 'But I take it that, as a result of what happened, the Hiltons are now divorced?'

'Yes.'

'Then I don't need to know anything else.'

'OK, let's leave that to one side for a while.' His voice was level. 'However, there is something else we must talk about.' He paused. 'Last night.'

'No,' she said quickly. 'Again, there's nothing to discuss. You were quite right,' she went on, the words squeezed from the tightness of her throat. 'I was scared and behaved badly. That's all there is to it and I—I can only apologise.'

There was a silence, then Jago said very quietly, 'As you wish.' His chair scraped across the floor as he rose. 'On second thoughts, it might be better if I didn't stay for breakfast. Thanks for the coffee.' He paused at the door, looking back at her, his mouth twisting cynically. 'And, of course, for the use of the sofa.'

And he was gone, leaving the house feeling empty and silent behind him.

CHAPTER THIRTEEN

WORK WAS THE thing. Work would fill all the echoing empty spaces. Remove the opportunities for thinking and the agony of a regret she could not afford.

Because I am better off without him, she told herself fiercely. I have to keep telling myself that until I believe it. And he was never mine, anyway. I must remember that too.

She rang a glazier who promised to be there before noon, then, teeth gritted, she flung herself into a whirlwind of housework.

By early afternoon, she had just unloaded the washing machine and was pegging towels and pillow cases on the line in the garden when she heard her father's voice calling to her, and turned to see him crossing the lawn.

He had a piece of paper in his hand, and she swore under her breath as she recognised the glazier's receipt, which she'd meant to put away.

'Well, my pet.' He hugged her. 'Been having a smashing time, I see. What's happened to the front door?'

She forced a smile. 'It's rather a long story.'

'I see.' He regarded her thoughtfully. 'Tea or something stronger?'

It was tea, drunk in a grassy corner shaded by fuchsias. Lloyd Denison listened to Tavy's hesitant, and strictly edited, account of events without comment, his face set in stern lines.

When she'd finished, he sat in silence for a while, then sighed. 'I never thought I would say this about anyone, my dear, but I'm actually glad neither Patrick Wilding or the Culham girl were born here, and therefore I did not christen them or prepare them for confirmation. If I had done so, I would feel I had failed.' He paused. 'But I'm glad Jago came to the rescue and you didn't have to be alone.'

Tavy bent forward and picked a daisy, twirling it between her fingers. She kept her face and voice expressionless. 'Yes, it was kind of him.'

'And what is this unpleasant surprise that young Wilding threatened? Do you have any idea?'

Tavy frowned. 'None at all. I wish I did.' She was silent for a moment, then roused herself determinedly. 'So, how did your trip go? Did you enjoy seeing Mr Castleton again?'

'Very much so. But it wasn't simply a pleasant break. I'm afraid I misled you over that. And Derek isn't plain Mister any more. He was appointed Bishop of Milcaster six months ago, and as the office of Dean has recently become vacant, he invited me over to offer it to me.'

She gasped. 'But that's wonderful—isn't it? What did you say?'

'That I would give him my answer in a few days.'

She frowned. 'After the Archdeacon's visit?'

'No, my dear. I'm not hoping for a stay of execution on Holy Trinity. Economics have spoken, I'm afraid. But I wanted a little time to think, and pray. And talk to you, of course.' He took her hand. 'Find out what you're planning to do with your life.'

'Well, I still intend to do a Bachelor of Education degree, but that can't happen till next year, so I can come with you to Milcaster, if you want me. Keep house for you there.'

She saw a slight shadow cross his face and said quickly, 'Unless there already is someone to do that.'

'Well, yes, darling.' He still looked troubled. 'The late

Dean was unmarried and his housekeeper is hoping to stay on, I think. She was with him for some years and seems a capable, pleasant woman. But I wasn't thinking of that. I'm more concerned about you.'

His fingers tightened round hers. 'Are you absolutely certain about teaching? You're not going to consider any other options?'

She looked down at the grass. 'They've always been a bit thin on the ground, at least round here. And I wouldn't want to stay, after what's happened.'

She shrugged. 'So, it's time for a complete break. And I'm sure I'll find something I can do in Milcaster.' She added brightly, 'It's almost an adventure.'

He said nothing, so she galloped on, 'Tell me about the Deanery. And the cathedral, of course. Does it have one of those old closes?'

'Yes, indeed. And the Deanery is charming, rebuilt in the early eighteenth century I'm told.'

He was silent for a moment. 'But so many years of our lives have been bound up in Hazelton Magna and I'd hoped…' He checked. 'But enough of that. I'm just sorry we'll be leaving on a sour note.' He paused again. 'I just wish I could feel more positive about your intentions.'

She managed a giggle. 'You mean the road to hell might be paved by them? I'll take care it isn't.'

Yet, as they walked back to the house, she discovered 'Easy, easy is the descent' throbbing in her brain with its raw, insistent beat, and continuing to haunt her for the rest of the day and late into the night.

Over breakfast the next morning, she said casually, 'I suppose we'd better start thinking what we're going to take with us when we move.'

Her father pulled a face. 'What a blood-curdling thought.'

'Then why don't you sort out your books and special things, and I'll do the rest?'

'Darling, you won't have time, not with your day job.'

She said carefully, 'Actually, I've decided to give that up. As we're going, I won't be able to see it through to the finish, and Jago will have more time to find a replacement.'

'But you haven't told him yet.' It was a statement not a question.

Tavy shifted uncomfortably. 'I'll telephone Barkland Grange later. But he may be away. He often is.'

'Of course. He's a very busy young man.' He smiled at her as he got up. 'And now, I must go and be busy at Morning Service.'

Even with the house to herself, Tavy was reluctant to make the call to Jago. The ironing had been done, the vegetables prepared and a chicken was roasting in the oven before she went to the telephone, hoping he would be elsewhere.

But found herself put straight through to his suite.

'Octavia,' he said. 'I had a feeling you would call, no doubt to tell me you're giving up your job.'

She said stiffly, 'Well, yes. You see—I won't be around.'

There was a silence, then he said, 'Running away, Tavy?'

'Not at all,' she denied quickly. *Maybe too quickly.* 'It's just that we'll be moving to Milcaster quite soon. My father's going to be the new Dean.'

'And you're going to be—what?' he drawled. 'The Dean's daughter serving tea to clergy wives, like something out of Trollope?'

She bit her lip. 'For a while. Until I can get on a teacher training course.'

'Ah,' he said. 'Then it seems I shall just have to let you go.'

She hesitated. 'I don't want to leave you in the lurch, so I could make sure the furniture arrives safely tomorrow.'

'That won't be necessary,' he said. 'Barbie is arriving later today. She'll see to it.' He paused. 'Unless, of course, you'd like to meet her.'

'Thank you,' she said, hoping he hadn't picked up her

swift intake of breath. 'But—no. I'm going to have a thousand things to do here.'

His voice was courteous. 'Then I mustn't keep you.'

'No,' she said again. 'Well—goodbye.' And put the phone down, her hand shaking.

After lunch, she decided to go into the garden for a little desultory weeding, which turned into a marathon.

She was just on her way back to the house for a cold drink when she met her father, holding an envelope.

'Someone called Charlie has just brought this for you, darling. Orders from the boss, he said.'

'He's Jago's chauffeur.' She shrugged. 'It's probably the equivalent of a P45.'

But inside the envelope was a cheque, and a note which read, 'For services rendered,' both signed 'Jago Marsh.'

She said her voice husky with disbelief, 'Dad—this cheque's for—two thousand pounds. I can't accept all that. Not when I only worked for such a short time.'

The Vicar said calmly, 'Of course you can, my dear. You were clearly a valued employee, and he's chosen to give you a bonus.'

'Then I shall put it in the charity box.'

'You will not,' her father said firmly. 'Remember how you worked at that school for a pittance. On this occasion charity can begin at home.' He patted her shoulder. 'Why not get away for a holiday somewhere. Buy yourself some new clothes too.'

He paused. 'You must thank him, of course.'

Tavy crushed Jago's note in her hand. She said tautly, 'I'll write to him.' And went indoors.

'Is the Archdeacon meeting us at the village hall?' Tavy asked as she and her father left the Vicarage on Wednesday evening.

'Apparently he's on his way. He seemed rather ill-

humoured when he rang yesterday. Asked if we'd been com-
plaining to the newspapers about Holy Trinity's closure. Of
course, I told him no.'

'Maybe we should have done,' Tavy said thoughtfully.
'Mounted a campaign.' She sighed. 'But it's too late now.'

'Oh, I don't know,' Mr Denison returned briskly. 'Maybe
the age of miracles isn't over yet.'

That, Tavy decided wryly, was being over-optimistic.

There'd been an odd atmosphere in the village this week,
she thought. And her feeling that conversations were being
terminated at her approach had intensified.

It was clear that the new presence at Ladysmere and her
own absence had been duly noted.

And only that morning she'd overheard June Jackson talking to another woman. 'New furniture arriving every day,'
she'd declared. 'And about the biggest mattress Ted's ever
seen. It took four of them to get it upstairs.' She chuckled.
'So you can tell what's on that gentleman's mind, all right.'

Tavy whisked round and went back the way she had come
before she was spotted. Her heart was hammering oddly,
but she told herself not to be so stupid. She knew perfectly
well that Jago was refurbishing the four-poster in the master
bedroom, and at the right moment, it seemed.

She hadn't yet thanked him for the cheque. She'd written several notes, each more stilted than the last, but had
sent none of them.

She would have much preferred to stay away from tonight's meeting, knowing it would only bring her more distress, when she was already struggling to maintain her usual
composure. But she knew she had to be there for her father's
sake, if for no other reason.

She had dressed neatly for the occasion in a navy skirt,
topped by a white blouse, and put her hair up into a tidy,
well-skewered knot on top of her head. So the surface was
calm and orderly at least.

The Archdeacon's car was already parked near the hall door when they arrived.

'Ready for a quick getaway, no doubt,' Tavy whispered to her father.

'I hardly think there'll be a lynch mob, darling,' he returned.

Yet there was certainly a mob. Nearly every seat was taken, and more chairs were being retrieved from the storage area under the platform. Looking round, Tavy saw faces she did not even recognise. She did however notice Norton Culham and his wife, sitting together, stony-faced.

The Archdeacon was standing at the front of the hall, talking to Mrs Wilding. He was a tall man, whose face seemed set in a perpetual vague smile. But this was misleading, because everyone in the diocese knew he was, in fact, the Bishop's hatchet man.

As Tavy and the Vicar walked towards them, Mrs Wilding moved hastily away, and joined Patrick who was seated, head bent, in the second row.

The Archdeacon's voice was cold. 'I see the meeting has attracted quite a crowd. I trust they are not hoping for a change of heart by the diocese.'

'Everyone is entitled to hope, Archdeacon,' Lloyd Denison returned evenly.

'Including yourself. A projected move to Milcaster as Dean, I hear. Laudable if a little ambitious under the circumstances.' The smile was positively vinegary. 'However, shall we start the meeting?'

Tavy watched them mount to the platform, aware of a sudden stab of anxiety. What on earth could the Archdeacon have meant? she wondered, looking round for an empty seat, only to find she was being beckoned to by a small woman, with iron grey hair cut in a severely uncompromising bob, and bright, if not sharp brown eyes, who was lifting a large, solid handbag off an adjoining chair to make room for her.

'So you're the Vicar's daughter,' she commented briskly as Tavy sat down. 'I recognise the hair.'

Tavy, faintly bewildered, was just going to ask, 'Have we met?' when the Archdeacon rapped on the table in front of him on the stage, called for silence and announced that proceedings would commence with a prayer.

As his sonorous tones invited the Almighty's guidance, Tavy heard a stir at the back of the hall and felt the excitement rippling through the crowded hall. She did not have to look. Not when awareness was shivering through her entire body. Besides, he'd said he would be there.

She stared straight ahead of her with eyes that saw nothing, listening as the Archdeacon spoke with well-modulated regret about the closure of Holy Trinity.

'A decision not taken lightly, but forced on us due to the dangerous dilapidation of the building, and the extortionate cost of putting it right.'

However, he added, arrangements would be made to hold regular acts of worship here in the village hall, including a monthly communion service.

Ted Jackson got to his feet. 'And who'll be doing that?' he asked. 'Will we be getting a new Vicar in place of Mr Denison?'

The Archdeacon paused. 'The needs of the parish will be met by members of our local team.'

The Vicar said gently, 'But presumably you would find a replacement for me if the church could be privately repaired.'

The Archdeacon's sigh sounded almost regretful. 'In times like these, there is little hope of that, I fear.'

'On the contrary,' said Mr Denison blandly. 'I have received an offer to cover the entire cost of renovation, on condition that the parish continues to function as in the past.' He took an envelope from an inside pocket of his coat and placed it on the table. 'Perhaps you would pass on the details to the Bishop.'

Shock wiped the fixed smile from the Archdeacon's face. 'An offer,' he repeated ominously. 'What possible offer is this and why have you waited until now to tell me?'

'By the time it was confirmed, you were already on your way.'

'And who has made this—offer?' The Archdeacon flicked the envelope almost disdainfully.

'I have.' And Jago walked to the front of the hall, ignoring the inevitable buzz that accompanied him.

From head to foot, he was in black again. He was even wearing the belt with the silver buckle that Tavy remembered from their first meeting.

He said, 'My name is Jago Marsh, and I'm making my home here in this village. Holy Trinity church is at the heart of this community, and I want that to continue. If money is all that's needed, I can provide it.'

The Archdeacon's tone was icy. 'I have heard of you, Mr Marsh. Your exploits in the world of rock music have made you notorious. I presume this is some quixotic attempt to re-establish yourself in normal society—even as Lord of the Manor perhaps.'

Jago shrugged. 'The original church was built by the family at Ladysmere. I am simply upholding their tradition.'

'I suppose you realise several hundred thousand pounds is required. Do you wish to bankrupt yourself?'

'I've no intention of doing so,' Jago returned. 'I've had an independent survey carried out, which indicates that, for some reason, the original estimates were far too high.'

As the murmur in the hall built, Mrs Wilding was on her feet. 'Even so, the offer cannot be considered, Archdeacon. The parochial church council will never agree.' She sent Jago a venomous look. 'This is tainted money from a man not fit to live near decent people.'

There was a concerted gasp and a voice from the back called, 'Steady on. No need for that.'

But Mrs Wilding swept on. 'And the Vicar, as I have told you, has been on familiar terms with him, and even allowed his own daughter to be corrupted by this—sexual predator.'

Horrified, Tavy tried to get to her feet in instinctive protest, but her neighbour's hand on her arm restrained her.

'Sit still, child. Let them have their say,' came a fierce whisper.

Mr Denison sat grimly silent, but the Archdeacon was looking totally aghast. 'Mrs Wilding—dear lady—I recognise that you have concerns, but there are laws against slander...'

Norton Culham got up. 'Not when there's truth to be told. And it's an open scandal what's been going on. The girl's a college dropout who can't hold down a proper job. She chased after Mrs Wilding's boy, but he wasn't interested, so she was probably flattered when a fellow with plenty of money started showing her a good time.

'And then she's up at the Manor, supposedly working.' He laughed unpleasantly. 'Working on her back, more likely. One room in the house fit to be used, and that's a bedroom all tarted up. My Fiona suspected what was going on and took a photograph of it. Then, she found a drawing he'd done of the girl, parading round in the altogether,' he added with relish. 'I have them here for anyone to see.'

'I would like to look at them.' It was Tavy's neighbour, holding out an imperious hand. Norton Culham passed them forward, and she took a quick glance and snorted.

'As I thought, my bedroom,' she said. 'And what right has your daughter or anyone else to invade my privacy taking snapshots? It is blatant intrusion. And the nude girl in the drawing looks to me like that vulgar statue down by the lake.'

She turned and scrutinised Tavy, stricken and blushing to the roots of her hair as she looked down at the sketch. 'But if it is this young woman, then Jago had better abandon any idea of a career in art, because I see no likeness at all. What do you say, Vicar?' She rose briskly and handed the drawing up to him.

'I agree with you, madam,' Mr Denison said quietly, taking a folded sheet of paper from his inside pocket, and opening it out. Tavy recognised it instantly as the sketch from the church, and her heart turned over. 'Now this is unmistakably Octavia, wouldn't you say, Archdeacon?'

The Archdeacon, looking as if he wished to be a thousand miles away, murmured something acquiescent.

'Just a minute,' Norton Culham said aggressively. 'Who's this woman, anyway?'

She turned slowly, giving him a piercing look. 'My name is Margaret Barber, and I was at one time Mr Marsh's nanny. I am now housekeeper at Ladysmere.' She added, 'And if you had ever been in my nursery, my good man, I would have taught you to be more civil,' then resumed her seat.

Barber? Tavy thought numbly. Could it be possible…?

She said in an undertone, 'Are you, by any chance— Barbie?'

'Yes—although it is a familiarity I do not generally permit on such brief acquaintance.' She gave Tavy a nudge. 'Now I think we should be quiet and listen.'

'Then if it's all so innocent, why was his Jeep outside the Vicarage all night last Friday when the Vicar was away?' Mr Culham was demanding. 'And him there still, half-dressed, on Saturday morning. You saw him, didn't you, Patrick?'

Patrick, his head buried in his hands, said nothing.

'I reckon that's enough.' It was Ted Jackson again. 'You've had a lot to say, Mr Culham, and none of it pleasant to hear, especially about a young lady we've all known and thought well of since she was in her pram.

'You have a daughter yourself,' he went on. 'And there's plenty some of us could say about her, if truth be known. But if anything were to happen to Mrs Culham, would your

Fiona come home and take care of you like Miss Tavy did with her father?'

He shook his head. 'Let's hope you don't have to find out.'

'As for Mr Jago.' He looked round the hall, grinning broadly. 'It's as plain as the nose on your face what's been going on there, and a sorry thing if a young man can't court the pretty girl who's taken his fancy without people thinking the worst.

'And if things went a bit far the other evening, I dare say the Vicar, knowing human nature as he does, won't be too hard on the pair of them.'

'No,' Tavy moaned silently, burning all over, and wishing only for the floor to open up and swallow her. 'Oh, please, don't let this be happening.'

Her father said gently, 'There'll be no strain on my tolerance, Mr Jackson. My daughter discovered on Friday that someone who shares Mr Culham's poor opinion of her had painted obscenities on our front door and broken a pane of glass. She was naturally distressed and Mr Marsh remained downstairs in the house overnight in case the vandal paid a return visit. That's all that happened.'

Norton Culham gave another jeering laugh. 'You expect me to believe that?'

'No, Mr Culham,' Lloyd Denison said with faint weariness. 'I have learned over the years that you are unlikely to believe anything I have to say either about this world or the next.' He shook his head. 'But I see no reason why you should doubt Mr Marsh.'

'I can tell you that, Vicar,' said Ted Jackson. 'He's taken against him because Mr Jago wouldn't sell him a field he wanted, having promised Jimmy Langtree he could graze his sheep there again, like he did when Sir George was alive. That's the top and bottom of it.'

There was a murmur of assent from the body of the hall. Upon which, the Archdeacon appeared to gather himself.

'I can see no useful purpose in prolonging this meeting,' he announced, picking up the envelope. 'I shall give this to the Bishop. I imagine he will wish to arrange a meeting with you, Mr—er—Marsh, to ensure among other things that you can guarantee this money.'

Jago smiled politely. 'I shall look forward to it.'

Oh, God, thought Tavy, when he turns, he'll see me. And I can't face him—not after all this.

She shot to her feet and, head bent, scurried up the aisle to the door and out into the small foyer. Where a voice halted her. 'Tavy.'

She turned reluctantly and found herself facing Patrick.

He came to her. His eyes looked heavy and raw as if he hadn't slept for weeks.

He said, 'You won't want to hear this, but I'm sorry. Sorry for everything that's happened.' He shook his head. 'You probably can't understand, but I loved Fiona so much I'd have done anything. Anything...'

Yes, thought Tavy. I can understand, only too well.

'And now she's gone—for good.' His voice shook. 'She sent me a bloody text to say so. I always knew that she didn't want to stay here and run the school like our parents planned. But I thought we'd be together—somewhere.'

He added with difficulty, 'I hated hearing them talk about you just now. I'll be leaving too, as soon as I find another job.'

He paused. 'But, Tavy, what I said about Jago and Pete Hilton's wife was true. He did go off with her. And maybe he was in love with her when it happened, but she's out of his life now. Forgotten.

'And the same could happen to you.'

She said quietly, 'I'll take great care not to allow that. Goodbye, Patrick,' and walked away into the evening sunlight, without looking back.

CHAPTER FOURTEEN

TAVY WAS SITTING at the kitchen table, an untouched cup of coffee in front of her, when her father returned.

She said, 'You didn't tell me.'

'About the offer?' The Vicar reached for the coffee pot and poured some for himself. 'My dear, each time I've mentioned Jago's name lately, you've changed the subject. Besides, it only became a certainty earlier this evening.'

'I see.' She took a breath. 'And did you know who Barbie really was?'

'Of course.' He added gently, 'He would have told you too, had you asked him. Why didn't you?'

She lifted her chin. 'Because it wasn't my business.'

He said calmly, 'In that case, you can hardly complain if you were kept in the dark.'

She gasped. 'You think it's all right for him to make a fool of me?'

'I think, darling, you've been making a fool of yourself.' He paused. 'I notice you didn't stay to thank him for what he's doing for the church.'

'I'm sure there were plenty who did. I wouldn't be missed.'

There was a silence, then he said almost harshly, 'It's at moments like this that I feel so totally inadequate without your mother.' He picked up his coffee. 'I'll be in my study.'

Tavy stared after him, her thoughts whirling. He had never spoken like that before. As if she had disappointed him.

She waited for five minutes, then followed him. He was sitting at his desk, his chess board in front of him, working out a problem.

'Dad, I'm in such a muddle.'

'Are you, my dear? Well, you're probably not alone in that.'

'For one thing, how can Jago possibly afford the repairs to the church, especially after buying Ladysmere, with all the cost of renovations and furnishings?'

'I gather Descent are getting together again to stage a farewell concert. He is donating his share of the takings.'

She gasped. 'But that can't be. He said that part of his life was over.'

'Clearly, he's changed his mind.'

'But the band won't be the same without Pete Hilton,' she protested. 'People may not go.'

'Jago tells me the original line-up will all be present.'

She said passionately, 'That's just not possible. Not after Jago destroyed his friend's marriage.'

The Vicar sent her a shrewd glance. 'I think the young man did that himself, my dear. But if you want a fuller explanation, you will have to ask Jago.' He moved a knight. 'I think you'll find him at the house.'

She didn't need the jacket she'd brought with her, she thought as she walked up the drive to Ladysmere. It was still very hot. She was about to ring the bell when she heard the faint sound of music on the still air, and instead walked round the side of the house to the rear terrace.

The French windows leading into the drawing room were standing open, and as Tavy approached, she recognised the music as Mozart's *Requiem*.

She stepped hesitantly inside, and stopped dead because the room was no longer just an empty space.

Two enormous, deeply cushioned sofas in sapphire blue

corded velvet now flanked the wide fireplace and a thick cream fur rug lay between them in front of the hearth.

Jago was lounging on the furthest sofa, his shirt unfastened to the waist, a cut glass tumbler containing some deep golden liquid in one hand, his face brooding, almost bitter.

She was sorely tempted to retreat, but made herself take another step forward. At that, he glanced up, his eyes narrowing in total astonishment as he stared at her, his body no longer relaxed but tense as a coiled spring.

She tried to smile. 'I seem to have startled you.'

'You have,' he said. 'I thought you'd be somewhere else entirely, enjoying the first stages of reconciliation. Or have you decided to make him wait?'

'What are you talking about?'

He said wearily, 'I'm not blind, Octavia. I saw Patrick Wilding follow you out of the hall, and when I came out, you'd both gone. I did say if you were patient, he'd realise what a fool he'd been. It seems I was right.'

'No.' She shook her head. 'You're utterly wrong. He came after me to offer an apology—of sorts. It's definitely over with Fiona, and he's planning to go away.'

'Well, don't worry. I'm sure he'll be back.'

'I sincerely hope not.' She hesitated. 'I've come here to ask you something.'

'Then you'd better sit down,' he said. 'I'm drinking single malt. Will you join me?'

'Yes,' she said. 'Please.'

His mouth twisted sardonically. 'It must be a hell of a question,' he observed as he switched off the music and left the room.

Tavy sat down on the opposite sofa. It was like sinking into a wonderful soft cloud, she thought, trying to marshal her thoughts.

'Delivered yesterday and about as far from dark brown

leather as it's possible to get,' Jago said, as he returned carrying a bottle and another tumbler.

'They're lovely,' she said, running a hand over the luxurious blue fabric. She shook her head. 'You don't waste time, do you?'

'Not when I find what I want,' he agreed, resuming his seat. He raised his glass. 'Cheers.'

She murmured a response, then sipped the whisky, cautiously savouring its smoky taste.

There was a silence, then he said, 'I'm listening.'

'My father tells me your band is getting together again. That's how you're raising the money for Holy Trinity.'

He nodded. 'If the Bishop will accept my tainted money. It's the farewell concert we planned a long time ago. And we're issuing a final album too. Pete and I have been working on it since I came back to Britain.'

She swallowed. 'Then he's forgiven you.'

'For what?' he asked wryly. He shook his head. 'It's myself I have to forgive.'

'I don't understand.'

He said tiredly, 'Why should you? It's all a world away from any experience of yours—or I hope it is.'

He paused. 'Descent's success was instant and meteoric. Everything—booze, drugs, girls—there for the taking. A time of total excess.' He gave a twisted smile. 'And we were—excessive.

'Then one day, you wake up and wonder what you're doing to yourself. You realise that nothing gives you a high like standing in some arena listening to the crowd go mad. And you take back your self-control and your self-respect.

'Only by then it was too late for Pete. My best mate had become an alcoholic and coke addict and I hadn't seen it happening. His marriage to Alison had already broken up. She was a lovely girl but she couldn't handle what he'd become.

She came to me for help, and I took her to her parents' home in Malaga, which probably started the rumours.

'Even after Pete agreed to go into rehab, his parents refused to believe that their quiet sensitive son was addicted to anything. And to them I was the bastard who'd led him into bad ways.'

He added wearily, 'And, in retrospect, perhaps they weren't so far from the truth. I should have seen he was more vulnerable than the rest of us—looked out for him.'

He was silent for a moment. 'Anyway, he's back with us now, still an alcoholic, of course, taking one day at a time, but totally off drugs. And planning to become a potter once Descent's swansong is finally over.'

'And Alison?' Tavy asked. 'What happened to her?'

He looked faintly surprised. 'Apart from the fact she divorced him, I haven't the slightest idea. She could hardly be expected to keep in touch. But why ask about her now and not the other day?'

She said, 'Because then I thought she was Barbie.'

He was very still suddenly. 'And if she had been? What then?'

She said, stammering a little, 'Well, it would have explained why you wanted to buy a house in a quiet backwater like this. To make a fresh start—with her.' She made a performance of looking at her watch. 'But I've taken up quite enough of your time.'

'No,' he said. 'You could never do that. And I think you know it.' There was a note in his voice that she found unnerving. 'Now let me ask you a question. Why did you run away after the meeting if it wasn't to Patrick?'

'You really thought I'd want anything more to do with him?'

'Why not?' He shrugged. 'Sometimes people go on loving the wrong person, in spite of everything, and though they know it will lead to misery. You told me so yourself.'

Colour rose in her face. 'But I didn't mean Patrick. You should have known that. I—I was speaking generally.' She took a deep breath. 'But I also ran away because I was embarrassed.'

His brows lifted. 'You don't think anyone believed the Wilding woman and Fiona's vile father?'

'No, I was thinking of Ted Jackson.' She looked down at her glass. 'I can't imagine why he said—what he did. About us. Because there isn't any us. I know that. Just you—being kind. You must have been mortified by his comments.'

'No,' he said. 'Not in the slightest. Because he was only wrong about one thing. He claimed everyone knew that I was courting you. Yet it seems to have missed you, the one most involved, by a country mile, even now, when it's been publicly pointed out.

'Of course,' he went on. 'You may be trying to find a tactful way of saying you wouldn't have me if I came gift-wrapped. But if not, maybe we could find some way of making this courtship slightly less one-sided.'

She said in a voice she didn't recognise, 'I don't understand.'

He put his glass on the floor beside him. 'Then try this.' His voice was almost harsh in its intensity. 'I love you, Octavia. I have done from the moment I saw you, and I always will. And I want to marry you and spend the rest of my life with you.'

'But that's not possible. We—we've only just met.' She was trembling violently, her voice husky. 'We hardly know each other…'

'Darling, you met Patrick Wilding a hell of a long time ago, and dated him for months, but what did you really know about him?'

'But you don't—you can't want me,' Tavy said wildly. 'Not when you sent me away the other night…'

'What else could I do?' Jago spread his hands. He said

very gently, 'Sweetheart, I wanted you like hell. You were a dream come true. But all the indications were that you were still in love with Patrick, and I couldn't bear the idea that I might only be a surrogate lover.

'Because there might have come a moment when you realised you were very definitely in the wrong arms, and I—I couldn't risk that. It seemed safer—wiser to send you away until I could be sure that you wanted me and no one else.

'Besides,' he added carefully. 'Neither the Vicarage carpet or a narrow single bed were the ideal options for the kind of seduction I had in mind. And since I was sure you weren't on the Pill, my having no protection was an additional factor.'

'Oh.' Tavy was blushing again.

'Oh, indeed,' he said and sighed. 'So I challenged you to take off your robe, knowing you wouldn't do it, any more than you'd have walked naked out of the lake that first time I saw you.'

He smiled at her. 'I walked back to the house in a daze that day, knowing that I'd be buying a home to share with you and no other.

'When I came to the Vicarage the next day, it was to give your father a frank rundown on my past, outline my future, and assure him that my intentions were entirely honourable.'

Tavy gasped. 'What on earth did he say?'

Jago's smile became a grin. 'He thought for a moment, then smiled and wished me luck.'

'He didn't mention Patrick?'

'Not a word. He left me to discover that for myself and suffer the tortures of the damned as a result. I'd never been jealous before and I didn't like it.'

'Yet you let me think that Barbie was your girlfriend…'

'In the vain hope that it might provoke some reaction. Yet you simply prepared her room as if her prospective arrival didn't bother you at all, instead of grabbing me by the throat and demanding to know what the hell was going on.'

She said breathlessly, 'But don't you see—I was scared to ask! Scared what your answer might be. It seemed better, somehow, not to know. As if that could somehow make me less unhappy.'

He said huskily, 'Oh, my dearest love.' He rose and came across to her, drawing her to her feet and cupping her face in his hands. 'Well, I'm prepared to take the risk. So, my wonderful, my precious girl, will you marry me?'

She slid her arms round his neck, feeling the dishevelled dark hair silken under her hands, smiling into the tawny eyes watching her with such tender intensity.

She said softly, 'Put like that—what can I do but say "Yes—and yes"?'

He said her name on a shaken breath and began to kiss her, gently at first and then with growing hunger, his mouth feasting on hers, her famished, untried senses responding in a kind of delirium.

She found her body leaning into his, as if wanting to be absorbed into the totally male hardness of bone and muscle. Knowing for the first time the overwhelming need to be joined, to become one with a man. Her man. Feeling the tight, cold knot of misery deep within her begin to dissolve in his warmth. In the strength of the arms holding her so closely, and the sensuous liquid fire of his kisses.

His hands slid down her body, tracing the length of her spine, and moulding the slender curve of her hips as he drew her even closer, awakening her to the potent demand of his arousal and all it signified.

His lips nibbled at her throat, gliding down to the opening of her shirt and pushing the fabric aside to reach the warm skin beneath.

Tavy felt her breasts swell against the confines of the lacy cups which encased them, her nipples hardening in anticipation of his caress—her first experience of such an intimacy, she thought, her senses drowning.

And yet this was also the beginning of a journey for which she was totally unprepared.

Jago, she knew, was accustomed to very different girls in his arms and his bed. Girls who would meet his demands and desires with their own.

Not someone who only had love to guide her and was suddenly scared that it might not be enough.

He lifted his head. 'What's wrong?'

'Nothing...'

'I don't think so.' He studied her flushed face. 'You were here with me, now you're not.'

She shook her head, looking down at the floor. 'It's stupid, I know. It's just that I've never...' And stopped, not knowing how to go on. Terrified that he might laugh at her.

He said huskily, 'Darling, you mustn't be frightened. But you have to want this too, not let me rush you into something you're not ready for.' He kissed her again, lightly, his lips just brushing hers. 'And if you want more time, I can be patient. We can just be—engaged. Tell our families, put a notice in the papers, buy a ring.'

He ran a caressing finger down the curve of her cheek. 'Now I'm going to open some champagne and we'll drink to our future before I take you home.'

She watched him walk out of the room. The man she loved who, by some miracle, loved her in return. And who, because his intentions were honourable, was coming back to drink wine with her, before he took her home.

Except—this was her home. She belonged here. She belonged to him, and she should have called him back, and told him so. Proved it to him beyond all doubt.

Instead, she'd let a fleeting uncertainty spoil a moment that would never return.

She turned restlessly and moved to the windows, looking across the terrace to the garden still glowing in the last of the evening sun. And beyond the lawns, sheltered by the tall shrubs, unmoving in the still air, was the lake.

The lake...

And suddenly she began to smile. She even laughed out loud. Kicking off her shoes, she walked across the sun-warmed flags, unbuttoning her shirt as she went, and dropping it at the head of the terrace steps.

Halfway across the lawn she paused, unzipped her skirt, stepped out of it and walked on, leaving it lying on the grass.

She draped her bra over the branch of a convenient buddleia, and negotiated a bank of fuchsias, just coming into bud, which brought her on to the edge of the lake.

The Lady was still there, gazing down into the waters, which had been cleared since Tavy's last visit, and were now reflecting back the turquoise, pink and gold streaks in the sky.

She whispered, 'Wish me luck,' as she slipped off her briefs and left them at the foot of the statue before wading in, taking her time, trailing her fingertips in the water as it got deeper.

She did not hear him arrive, but she knew the moment he was there just the same. She turned slowly, standing motionless for a long moment to let him look at her, before lifting her hands to take the clip from her hair and shake it loose over her shoulders. And wait.

Jago's face was taut, the tawny eyes burning. He said hoarsely, 'Octavia—oh God, you're so beautiful.'

She walked back to the bank, smiling at him, not hurrying, then stepped up into his arms.

His hands trembled slightly as they touched her, tracing her shoulders, her rounded up-tilted breasts, her delicate ribcage and tiny waist as if she was some infinitely precious and delicate porcelain figurine that a moment's clumsiness might shatter for ever.

He knelt suddenly, pressing his face against the flatness of her abdomen, his hands clasping her hips.

He said, his voice muffled, 'Now I'm the one who's scared.'

'No.' Tavy stroked the hair back from his forehead. 'How can you be?'

He looked up at her. 'Because this is the first time I've ever been in love. I didn't realise how I would feel. How perfect I would want it to be. For you. This first time.'

She knelt too. Kissed him on the mouth, aware of the first sweet stir of pleasure as his lips parted and she felt the slow, hot glide of his tongue against hers.

Jago's hands moved to her breasts, cupping them, his thumbs teasing her nipples until they stood proud. He lowered his head and took each of them into his mouth in turn, laving each erect, sensitive peak gently but with total deliberation, and Tavy felt a quiver of response run the length of her body and resonate in her loins with piercing, unequivocal need that shocked her by its force.

Her head fell back and a gasp escaped her as his fingers tangled in her hair, bringing her mouth back to his, in a deep and passionate kiss that left her languid and drained.

He turned her in his arms, lowering her to the ground, but instead of cool, crisp grass, she felt a rich and comforting softness against her bare flesh, and realised she was lying on the rug they'd used for their candle-lit picnic.

Jago took her back into his arms, and she stretched herself against him, revelling in the graze of his hair roughened chest against her excited nipples, slipping her hands inside his shirt and running her hands over his wide, muscled shoulders.

He'd said once he worked out, and she could believe it.

She heard herself say in a voice she hardly recognised, 'You're such a gorgeous shape.'

He said huskily, 'And you, my sweet, are Paradise.'

Because his hands were discovering her too, exploring every slender curve and delicate hollow, his lips following the intricate, enticing path of his fingers, awakening sensations she'd never been aware of until that moment. Feelings that turned her bones to water, and her blood into a warm tide in her veins.

And made her want so much more, especially when, as now, his hand was cupping her hip bone and straying with tantalising slowness down to her thigh. Where it lingered, his fingers gentle as a breeze on her sensitised skin.

Deep within her she felt a shaft of desire so piercing that she almost cried out aloud.

Her body was slackening, turning to liquid under the sensuous incitement of his touch. Only it wasn't enough, she thought, suppressing a tiny moan.

And then his hand moved, gentling its way between her parted thighs to the scalding inner heat of her with innate mastery, finding the tiny sensitive bud between the silky folds of woman flesh and circling on it slowly and delicately with a fingertip, until he had brought it to swollen, aching arousal.

And then, when she thought she could bear no more, she felt his fingers penetrating the slick hot wetness of her, thrusting into her with sure rhythmic strokes, taking her with relentless purpose towards some undreamed-of brink.

Her body arched towards him, the breath catching in her throat, the last vestiges of control slipping away as her whole being concentrated blindly on the spiral of exquisite agony building so inexorably inside her. She could hear herself moaning, voluptuously, pleadingly, and thought she heard him whisper, 'Yes.'

Then as his clever insistent fingers took her over the edge, and her body convulsed in the first sexual release it had ever known, her voice splintered and she cried out his name.

Afterwards, she cried a little and Jago held her, kissing

her mouth and wet eyelashes, whispering words that would live in her heart and memory for ever.

The echoes of the pleasure he had given her were still reverberating deep within her, making her long for more, kindling a renewed and urgent response to his lips. Wanting to return the joy.

But as her hands were reaching, fumbling a little, for the silver buckle on his belt, Jago stopped her, saying softly, 'Not here, not now, darling. It will be dark and much colder soon, and I want you in bed with me not pneumonia.'

She found herself wrapped warmly in the rug and lifted into his arms as he strode back towards the house, ignoring her not-too-serious protests and demands to be put down.

'And ruin one of my favourite fantasies about you? No chance.' He dropped a kiss on her tangled hair. 'This is the Spanish pirate in my ancestry.'

And when they reached the bedroom, laughing and breathless, the waiting four-poster was another revelation, heaped with snowy pillows, the crisp sheets half-concealed by a sumptuous black and gold satin coverlet.

'You did all this?' Tavy gasped as Jago put her down on the bed's yielding softness, and gently unwrapped her from the rug.

He shook his head. 'No, amazingly, it was Barbie—just before she announced that Charlie was driving her to Barkland Grange for the night. As I've mentioned, she's always been a law unto herself.'

Tavy watched him strip quickly, her eyes widening as she saw him naked. Her imagination had never taken her this far, and what she saw made her feel momentarily nervous, even a little daunted.

But the warmth and strength of his arms was a reassurance as he drew her to him, and as he began to kiss and caress her again, there was no place or reason for doubt.

In return, her hands scanned every inch of his lean, hard

contours, her fingers tracing the long supple spine down to his flat male buttocks and muscled flanks before sliding across his hip to begin a more intimate exploration, her touch tentative at first but growing bolder as Jago softly groaned his pleasure.

And when the moment came, she helped smooth the protective sheath over his erection before guiding him into the welcome of her desire-damp body, taking him more deeply with every thrust, rising and falling with him in love's eternal rhythm.

Experiencing once more with even sharper intensity the dizzying ascent to rapturous fulfilment, and hearing his cry of ecstasy echoing her own as he too reached his climax.

Afterwards they lay, making plans in between slow sweet kisses.

Jago went downstairs to fetch the champagne, still waiting to be opened, and brought it back with her clothes which he'd collected from the garden, explaining it was to save Ted Jackson's blushes.

'And I rang your father,' he added. 'Said we'd see him tomorrow.'

'Oh.' Tavy took an apprehensive gulp of champagne. 'What did he say?'

'Sent you his love and told me he was off to borrow a shotgun.' Jago slid back into bed. 'I'm only marrying you to have him as a father-in-law. I hope you know that.' He paused. 'And Mum and Dad will be delirious. A first grandchild in Oz and a daughter-in-law all in one year.'

'Isn't it lovely?' Tavy said. 'Making people happy.'

Jago smiled at her. 'Speaking of which,' he said, and took the champagne glass gently but firmly from her hand.

* * * * *

#3221 ENTHRALLED BY MORETTI
by Cathy Williams
Despite her lies, billionaire Alessandro Moretti wants Chase Evans in his bed, and isn't above blackmail to get her there. But will his punishing regime of red-hot revenge backfire as his increasing desire for Chase threatens his legendary self-control?

#3222 AN EXCEPTION TO HIS RULE
by Lindsay Armstrong
Harriet Livingstone only took attractive yet arrogant Damien Wyatt up on his job offer because she was desperate, but keeping their relationship out of the bedroom is becoming a battle—one neither of them seems to want to win....

#3223 THE WOMAN SENT TO TAME HIM
by Victoria Parker
Feisty Serena Scott knows that gorgeous world-class racing driver Finn St George is trouble with a capital 'T'.... But when Finn causes one scandal too many, it's up to Serena to get this shameless lothario back on track!

#3224 WHAT A SICILIAN HUSBAND WANTS
The Irresistible Sicilians
by Michelle Smart
Grace Holden tried to escape her past, but now she's back within Luca Mastrangelo's reach and discovering new depths to the man she married. Can she find the strength to fight the desire still blazing between them?

YOU CAN FIND MORE INFORMATION ON UPCOMING HARLEQUIN® TITLES, FREE EXCERPTS AND MORE AT WWW.HARLEQUIN.COM.

HPCNM0214RB